BUDS

By

James H Longmore

A HellBound Books Publishing LLC Book
Austin TX

James H Longmore

A HellBound Books LLC
Publication

BY JAMES H LONGMORE

HORROR
Blood & Kisses
'Pede
Tenebrion
Flanagan

BIZARRO
The Erotic Odyssey of Colton Forshay
Buds
And Then You Die
Feeder
I Am Joe's Unwanted Penis

James H Longmore

SOMETHING BY MEANS OF A PROLOGUE

Manchester, England. 1892

A thick, cloying blanket of industrial fog hung over the freak show tent as if attempting to conceal the abominations that skulked within. A frigid northern wind whistled in off the moors to tug at guide ropes and flap loose canvas wherever it could find purchase. The tent was long, squat, and huddled up next to the Big Top that housed the more wholesome delights the circus had to offer: like it was some bastard child desperate for acceptance.

A solitary figure braved the chilled, piercing wind to approach the tent, a thick woolen coat wrapped snugly about his tall frame. He was Lord Bartholomew Robertson, a well-to-do gentleman from a moneyed family who had made their fortune from the very same dark, satanic mills immortalized by William Blake. Robertson worked on occasion in the thriving family business, but much preferred to spend his time and generous salary on more adventurous pursuits.

Skirting around the periphery of the bigger tent, Robertson's ears were all of a sudden assaulted by the sounds of a thousand voices *oohi*ng and *ahhhi*ng, gasping and cheering at the no doubt thoroughly entertaining show within. However, Lord Bartholomew Robertson Esq. had little desire to watch performing elephants, preposterous clowns and men in gaudy red jacket-coats who sported ludicrous mustaches and tormented tigers with whips and chairs.

Robertson fingered his own 'tache - it was a most magnificent handlebar - waxed to perfection - and considered for a moment that for the little he cared for such circus fripperies, he did find the lady trapeze artists most alluring in their tight, glittering bodices and flimsy attire, and the contortionist girls were always a dream to behold. He'd paid for some time with one of the latter a good many years ago, back when such dalliances had been enough to sate his increasingly perverse desires. Nowadays, he considered such pleasures workaday and would most likely struggle to maintain his tumescence.

He still recalled with fondness the contortionist girl; he had happened upon her in some dark recess of a bazaar in Calcutta when he had been a much younger man out to experience the world and all of its depraved delights. The contortionist had been a mere three years into her twenties and had a petite, lithe body that she could fit with ease into a glass box no more than two feet square. Her body had not been underdeveloped, as with some he'd seen (he had no desire for performers who looked like ten-year-old boys, thank you very much!); her breasts were pert and firm with the most delightful rosebud nipples, and her hill of Venus was plump and concealed beneath a lustrous tangle of the blackest, silkiest hair one could ever have imagined.

How ardent the contortionist girl had been to accommodate: quite literally bending over backward to please her generous benefactor. She'd bow her infinitely flexible body so that the crown of her head touched her firm buttocks, and thus presenting her moist fleshpot to the gentleman. And there she'd stand as Robertson lapped away at her like an eager bee at a wonderfully exotic flower. She'd then wrap her body around his to meld into his skin with hers and would displace her limb joints to stimulate his whore-pipe with her nimble hands and feet whilst he penetrated her hot, wet flesh.

Of all of the contortionist's tricks – Robertson's favorite, the one that had him going back to her on many occasions, was where she would raise up her slim, honey-toned legs and hook her dainty feet behind her head. Then, she would curve her back and bend her body forwards until her vivacious breasts were squashed quite flat against her navel. From that seemingly impossible position, the girl would lick at her own Cupid's furrow with her expert tongue whilst Robertson engaged in congress with her. Whilst the girl's tongue flicked around Robertson's penetrating shaft and her own deliciously swollen, pink sex with its delicate bud: the girl would look deep into his eyes and smile her lascivious smile.

There were occasions when Robertson's contortionist would force her head ever so slightly further, so as to lick at her own brown rose whilst he was inside her womanhood. This provided the added delirium of a tongue stimulating him from within her puckered anus and the sensation of his penis rubbing against her pretty face.

And then on the occasion that was, by happenstance, to be their last coupling, Robertson had – in the throes of the most spectacular climax – pushed down on the contortionist's head and snapped her spine as surely as one would a kindling stick. He'd heard the resounding *crack* and saw the dislodged vertebrae erupt into an ugly, bruised knot between her shoulders, and to his everlasting shame; Robertson had ejaculated copiously inside the girl a second time.

To Robertson's horror, the contortionist hadn't died. She'd let out a guttural grunt when her body broke and crumpled into a flaccid heap when he'd pulled out of her; his seed had oozed from her hole like cream filling from an exotic pie and was soaked up by her silken hair. She'd struggled from the bed; her body wracked with great, heaving sobs, and had attempted to crawl away from Robertson – propelling herself forward on muscular arms and trailing the useless half of her broken body behind her. As she maneuvered away, the poor girl left behind a fat smear of excrement that had spilled out from her orifice without her feeling it.

The girl's owners had told Robertson the money he had paid by means of handsome compensation would go toward taking care of the girl in her newly crippled state and that he was not to worry as they would make his indiscretion go away. However, upon making inquiries when he revisited India some twelve months later, the contortionist was nowhere to be found, and the owners had denied to his very face any knowledge of the girl.

After that sorry incidence, Robertson had lost interest somewhat and, as with everything else in his two score years and five, the Lord had quickly grown tired of contortionists and their seemingly unbound flexibility and had sought out other, ever more perverse carnal activities.

And it was the pursuit of such activities that had brought him to this God-forsaken place on such a dreary night – for circus entertainment that was strictly not of the family variety.

Robertson ducked between the stiff canvas flaps of the sideshow tent. He'd given a cursory glance at the tent's exquisitely painted banner to make doubly certain that he was in the right place:

THE DELECTABLE NANCY & GRACE – SIAMESE TWINS EXTRAORDINAIRE

Upon entering the dim, dank confines of the tent, Robertson removed his top hat, as was protocol when in the presence of a lady – or, more appropriately, *ladies.*

Nancy bid her customer a very good evening. Her conjoined sister, Grace, followed the genteel greeting, and they invited Robertson to join them on their expansive bed with a sweeping gesture of the three arms they shared. Mesmerized by their exquisite beauty, Robertson did as instructed, and not once did he take his eyes away from the perfection of their naked *body.*

The twins were entirely identical; their skin was an exotic mid-tan with underlying grayish tinges that alternately darkened and lightened beneath the flickering light of the myriad candles struggling to illuminate the tent. Robertson saw their bodies were fused together from the base of their elegant necks down to the curve of the hips. There, the twins' united body once again separated into four honey-toned, shapely legs that spread out before them on the bed. Nestled between each pair of legs, Robertson espied their sensual love cracks. Each one glistened and pouted beneath luxuriant dark hair and was flanked by two further – fully formed, and one would presume entirely serviceable – vaginas, one at the very top of each inner thigh.

Nancy/Grace each had an arm growing as one would expect from their respective shoulders, along with a third one – as functional as its companions – which snaked from beneath the four weighty, pendulous breasts that swung proudly on the twins' shared chest. Of the breasts themselves, the outer two sported twin faces, each of which was beautifully hairless with hazel eyes that twinkled with wicked promise and mouths that gaped wide with sharp, glinting teeth.

Robertson fidgeted with his hat; it felt quite heavy in his nervous hands. He'd placed it upon his lap in an effort to hide the expanding erection that bulged in his breeches. It was peculiar, he thought, how he felt so awkward in the presence of the exquisite creatures, especially since there was no secret as to his purpose there. He was, however, pleased – more than – with his selection. Nancy/Grace was indeed a most delightful indulgence in every way.

Robertson inhaled deeply to better take in the heady scent of the twins' perfumed bodies and delightfully odorous, oozing sex. As he did so, his eyes meandered across the milky landscape of the body they shared: the pert, rose-red nipples, the smooth flatness of the belly with its mirror-image navels, and quickly down to the thicket of tousled pubic hair that matched the cascading, flame-red thatch upon their heads. Theirs was an unashamed hirsuteness that Robertson found to be almost unbearably arousing.

Nancy/Grace smiled at their client and slid across the rough woolen blankets to tease him with their proximity.

"How do you do?" Robertson asked politely.

"I am most please to make your acquaintance, ladies. My name is –"

They quieted him with the forefinger of their shared hand upon his lips, and in the silence, they began to undress him.

Lord Robertson was a well-known figure amongst the Europe-wide freak show community. It was a kinship in which, for a few Guineas, a properly connected gentleman could have his wicked way with the strange and exotic exhibits. Of course, this was not something the show's management widely publicized, but for those who moved in the right circles, it was easy enough to make the right connections. Robertson had traveled the length and breadth of the continent to seek pleasures with ever more bizarre specimens of humanity, never shy of delving into the deepest corners of depravity to do so. Amongst the many, he had sampled the delights of a genuine wolf woman in Prague, a be-scaled unfortunate in Vienna, a quadruple amputee girl in Paris, a young man blessed with multiple penises in Bucharest, and a true hermaphrodite in Barcelona. Somewhat predictably, each sordid tryst resulted in Robertson lusting for more and ever-hungry to find the next even more perverse coupling.

Perhaps, he mused, *this was to be the finest yet?*

Robertson was soon undressed and sitting quite comfortably on the edge of the conjoined twins' bed – perfectly naked save for his socks. Nancy/Grace clambered from the bed and stood before him. They took a firm hold of his head with all three of their hands and pressed it into their four fleshy bosoms; they seemed to delight in the loud sigh that elicited from him. The quaking, fleshy mounds enveloped Robertson's head, and he felt the wet mouths of the breast-heads as they sucked eagerly at his cheeks.

Robertson reached his arms around the twins' body to stroke their smooth, tanned skin with trembling fingertips. He paused to caress the large, bony lump he found in the middle of the ladies' back, a most delightful deformity 'til now hidden from him. The lump had a rough, malleable texture and seemed strangely *alive* beneath his touch. As Robertson's fingers played across its surface, he imagined he felt shifting, *moving*, as if something mysterious and indescribably erotic lurked just beneath the skin.

Nancy/Grace knelt before their charge and took his tumescent penis into first one mouth and then the other as they play-fought for control of the man's impressive member. At that moment, Robertson was self-consciously aware of his diseased manhood with its ulcerated shaft and pungent discharge that offended even his nose. He'd caught something decidedly unpleasant in a small town due North of Reykjavik a month or so previous from an interesting specimen with a huge, gaping hole where her face should have been and her internal digestive organs in a floppy, membranous sac on the outside of her body – just beneath her pubescent breasts. Within days of their coupling, Robertson had experienced a burning sensation whenever he urinated, and a bile colored discharge that stank like he was rotting from the inside had begun to ooze from the tip of his cock. Unfortunately, the mercury treatment he had been paying so handsomely for since his return didn't appear to be having much effect.

Robertson had no cause for concern, however. Both Nancy and Grace didn't seem to mind at all. In fact, they lapped fervently at the discharge, along with the clear fluid that seeped from his ulcerated member, and declared with sensual smiles it was of a most agreeable palate. The twins then kissed one another with Robertson's penis sandwiched between their four lips and their tongues gently caressed each other along with the twitching shaft between.

Robertson closed his eyes and lolled his head backward. He was totally immersed in the moment with the pleasures of the twins' eager tongues as they worked on him with their wet, full-lipped mouths

Abruptly, Nancy/Grace halted their work and stood up with a graceful coordination that belied their odd configuration. They clambered back onto the bed. Nancy/Grace pulled gently on Robertson's arms to bid him to lie down, all the while smiling their serene and miraculously identical smiles.

The rough bed covers grated against Robertson's back, but far from dampening his ardor, the primitive feel of the cloth served only to stoke it further. The Lord's penis stood to angry attention at its customary 45-degree angle – rock solid and glistening with the Siamese twins' saliva.

As Robertson watched, he noted with desire that Nancy/Grace maneuvered with astounding agility to position Grace's womanhood over its target. He moaned out loud as the wiry red tangle of hair tickled his sensitive tip, and then bit his lower lip as the warm juices of Grace's inner flesh stung his ulcerated shaft as slowly – ever so slowly – her pleasure pit folded around his cock and sucked him so deep inside he could feel the rubbery nub of her cervix nudging against him.

Robertson looked on with fascination as he slid deep into Nancy/Grace's unified body. With the muted light of the tent, he could see uncountable tiny faces atop rough, wart-like bumps secreted within the forest of copper hair around the twins' fleshpot. Each of those miniature faces had a pair of pin-prick, twinkling eyes and a small, yawning mouth that vomited forth a brownish-yellow, viscous fluid that served to further lubricate his coupling and add to the cloying, piscine stink that oozed from the Siamese twins. He could also see – and *feel*, much to his sexual delight – the two denuded thigh-borne pleasure pits rubbing against his legs to create warm, slippery trails and slurp at his flesh like twin, toothless mouths.

As Nancy/Grace rode the Lord gently, their four legs worked in unison to slide him in and out of Grace's vagina, and Robertson delighted as their trio of busy hands toyed with the four magnificent breasts swaying above him. As they fornicated, Robertson began to feel a strange fatigue wash over him as the pressure began to build in his groin; he began to fear he would not be able to contain himself for much longer, and his ecstasy would be over all too soon.

Then, suddenly, Nancy/Grace lifted up on their knees, and Robertson slipped out of Grace's hot vagina with a wet, slurping sound. As his penis slipped from her body, he felt a prickling sensation along its length as the tiny mouths upon the myriad Lilliputian faces nibbled at him with razor teeth. Suffice to say, even though they drew tiny droplets of blood, Robertson found the sensation most pleasurable.

The conjoined whores performed a graceful choreography with their four lithe legs, and in the blink of an eye, it was Nancy's dripping mot that was inviting Robertson to savor its heated delights. Once again, he found himself immersed in the overwhelming pleasures the twins brought to his every sense, and, once again, he felt himself dragged down into a pit of lethargy that felt not unlike the post-coital lassitude which often befell him *after* his inevitable climax. The Lord looked up at his muse, and to his fatigued eyes their outline blurred as he strained to focus upon their handsome faces; to Robertson it felt as if the very act of intercourse was *draining* his body's energy out through his penis.

Suddenly, a claustrophobic panic swept through Robertson. He struggled to sit up and balance himself precariously on his elbows. Nancy/Grace smiled down at him, oblivious to his alarm, and continued to grind on his crotch; their vile juices bubbled out to mix with his, making him slick and glistening wet.

Robertson fought the exhaustion that threatened to drive him in to a deep sleep and he sat himself all the way up. As he threw his arms around Nancy/Grace's midsection for support, his hands closed around the hard lump on their back.

The mysterious lump moved beneath Robertson's touch in a wriggling, shifting motion, and Robertson felt a sharp pain as razor teeth snapped at his hand and clean sheared off three of his fingers.

It bit me!

Robertson's mind screamed, although his voice was silenced through the shock of the assault. He struggled violently beneath the immobilizing weight of the bodies that sweated and ground on top of his. He kicked his legs and bucked like those crazy-eyed broncos at the Wild West shows, and, as he flailed his arms around like a madman, the ragged stumps on his left hand sprayed the conjoined twins with bright splashes of blood.

"Let me go!" Robertson wailed. "You confounded freaks!"

Two heads shook in unison. Three hands caressed the four breasts, painting them with smeared blood.

Robertson renewed his exertions, and although it went against every part of his Gentleman's code, he slapped hard at the pendulous breasts his bloodied handprints joining theirs across the ripe nipples. With each slap, Nancy/Grace twisted their body around with force, and Robertson saw in profile the horror that had erupted from their back.

It was a human face!

Still the twins writhed and ground against him, their ecstasy increased as their client's energies dwindled; as if his manic efforts to be free were exacerbating their own pleasures. Robertson screamed out loud and contorted his tormented body with renewed vigor as a sharp, gnawing pain shot through his thighs; the cock-traps on Nancy's inner thighs – at first so pleasurably warm and succulent – had sprouted teeth and were biting into his legs as Nancy clamped him firmly between hers. And, inside her exquisite body, he could feel a dozen tiny, clawed hands raking at his trapped manhood, shredding its bulging flesh until his blood flowed thickly from her and soaked into the bed.

As he struggled in vain, Robertson felt the vagina mouths chew their way through the skin, muscle, and sinew into his femoral arteries. As the warm flood of blood gushed out of him, Robertson imagined he could feel the hellish mouths' hot breath against the exposed meat of his thighs and he could hear their muffled laughter.

Once more, Robertson struggled against Nancy and Grace: his weakening, flailing limbs ragged up the bed covers and his wounded hand flopped wetly against something hard that was secreted beneath the covers – he yelped in pain like a kicked dog.

The thing—as long as his forearm, cylindrical with a curious bulge at one end—was not as heavy as it appeared to be. It was shiny black and constructed of a substance unfamiliar to Robertson's world-weary eye, but reminded him of the waxy beetle carapaces on the specimens his father had pinned inside the display cases in the library of his childhood. Atop the bizarre contraption was a dial of sorts that glowed with an eerie green light; adjacent to that, '*#1*' was stenciled in white.

The odd apparatus toppled from the twin's bed out of Robertson's sight and clattered to the floor with an alien, brittle, crunching sound; it shattered into a half-dozen jagged pieces.

Nancy/Grace froze. They stared down at the floor by the side of the bed, where Robertson supposed the strange item had fallen. They had a look of unadulterated rage on their faces. And then, the surface of their shared body erupted with dozens more arms, legs, and heads with faces that snarled at him through tiny, ragged teeth. Innumerable clawed fingers groped and tore at Robertson's face and body, tearing away his lips and tongue, ripping his flesh away in thick bloodied gobs.

Robertson's whole being was ablaze with the agony of the violations forced upon it, and he could feel every nerve ending scream out as clumps of skin, muscle, and organs were torn away. There was nothing he could do to defend himself against the enraged onslaught as Nancy/Grace had drained so much of his spirit with their hellish pleasure pits; so he watched helplessly as the once mesmerizingly beautiful twins sprouted ever more fat, succulent buds that forced themselves out through smooth, olive skin in spurts of viscous, stinking juices to reveal superfluous limbs and hideous, sneering faces.

It was a mercy when Nancy/Grace tore out Lord Robertson's eyes. At least that way, he was spared watching the abomination into which the twins had transformed tearing his helpless body asunder as it sucked his life and his very soul out through his penis. Robertson also didn't have to witness the satisfied smirk on their many faces as – perversely – he climaxed inside their conjoined body as life abandoned him.

THE FIRST PART OF OUR STORY

CHAPTER ONE: 0.003

San Diego, US. Present Day.

So, time travel had turned out to be a bit of a disappointment.

Wildus Guidry ran a nervous hand through his hair and stared blankly at the LCD gauge on the fat, black plastic tube that sat impotently on his basement floor.

At least the experiment had ostensibly been a success, he told himself, as he watched several jet-black strands of his hair float downwards to rest on the device. The thing *had* gone back in time, albeit a most unspectacular three one-thousandths of a second.

Guidry cast his weary eyes around the laboratory he'd built in the spacious basement of the vast family home he'd inherited five years ago at the tender age of thirty-one but could barely afford to run. The laboratory was cluttered with half-finished projects, tangled snakes of colored wires, and long-forgotten electrical appliances with their guts torn out and spread across the cold concrete – all testimony to the family fortune he'd squandered trying to invent something meaningful, something *worthwhile*. Guidry shuffled his bulky, muscular frame backward until the back of his knees touched the battered, tan leather office chair in which he did most of his thinking.

He sat down.

Guidry plucked the thick-rimmed, designer glasses from his face and rubbed at his eyes with a rough hand. He tried to tell himself that he should be happy to have finally achieved the scientific Holy Grail, but this felt like a hollow victory, one big fucking let-down.

From the start he'd forgone the notion of attempting forward time travel. Even as idealistic as Guidry was, he knew full well that one couldn't conceivably go someplace that hadn't existed; to him, that was akin to expecting to take a trip in a car that was still iron ore in a mountainside. However, when it came to backward travel, the past *had* happened and did exist somewhere. That had always been a distinct possibility in Guidry's mind.

He sighed, wished 'Chelle was down there with him to offer her consoling bosom or maybe even a blow job to take the sting out of his disappointment. Guidry's girlfriend's oral technique never failed to cheer him up; something in the way she rolled his dick end between her tongue and teeth drove him fucking batshit crazy.

He contemplated the time travel device once more, not ready to pick it up just yet – as if he would catch more disappointment from the act of touching the thing. He'd constructed it from the outer case of a *Fucklight*; an unsubtly named masturbation aid 'Chelle had bought for him; the thing was designed to resemble an ordinary flashlight (supposedly for discretion's sake) and had a rubbery inner sleeve that emulated the inner flesh of a pussy; it came in pink and brown, vagina, ass, and mouth styles.

Actually, 'Chelle had bought two of the infernal things – one each – and had insisted they play together. Guidry was forced to admit it was hot watching 'Chelle lick and finger the fleshy inside of the toy as if it were her lesbian lover, but he wasn't so keen on fucking his toy whilst she watched. Not that her watching him slide his cock into the fake slippery cunt was the problem, it was more that the thing felt to Guidry like he was sticking his dick into a Saran-wrapped jellyfish (*there* was something he'd never do again – who'd have thought they could sting through Saran Extra Tough?). He guessed that 'Chelle would most likely chew him a new one when she found out he'd used their toys, but the *Fucklight*'s tough plastic case, it transpired, was just the right size and perfect for protecting the delicate electronics that made time travel possible.

The device sat motionless on the floor where it had returned after spending an entire sixty seconds in the past. He'd programmed the thing to return after one minute after learning the hard way with his first prototype. With that one, Guidry had *expected* that its timeline would simply catch up, and he'd stood and stared at that very spot on the basement floor for two hours before realizing that something had gone spectacularly awry with his hypothesis. So, Prototype One was – literally – lost in the mists of time and floating around out there somewhere.

Thanks to his hindsight, at least Number Two had returned. Although, given the data it had brought back with it, Guidry was beginning to wish that the motherfucking thing hadn't bothered.

"Are you coming up for bed, or what?" Michelle Tran's husky voice broke Guidry's reverie.

There was impatience in her voice that made Guidry snap his head around with well-trained obedience.

"I *really* don't want to have to start without you," Michelle – '*Chelle* – purred, "Again."

'Chelle was mouth-wateringly stunning, even more so in the red latex body paint with which she had decorated her incredible body. For her man's benefit, she had painstakingly painted onto herself a rubber dress that began with a wide collar and covered her entire body down to her ankles, all apart from her delightfully pert D-cup breasts, which swung free and jiggled in liquid motion as she descended the stairs to the basement. Every curve of 'Chelle's tall frame was enhanced by the shiny material that served as her second skin. Guidry could see she had taken the time – and inordinate amount of patience – to paint her outer pussy lips glistening red and leave her inner labia quite bare; they pouted pink and moist through the latex like some timid sea creature. 'Chelle had covered her slender arms with armpit-length black latex gloves that shone and bulged tight over her biceps, and on her feet she wore six-inch, black stripper shoes that looked brand new.

Guidry's breath caught in his throat and he felt his dick tingle in his pants. 'Chelle had gone to a hell of a lot of trouble to seduce him tonight, no doubt a by-product of the amount of time he'd been spending on his work of late. The latex body paint was 'Chelle's latest favorite sex thing, and although it was a marvel – what outfits, bikinis, bodysuits and such she could create with the variety of paints she had at her disposal – the preparation was time-consuming and meticulous. For example, before she would even begin with the paint on her hot body, 'Chelle would remove every single one of her body's hairs, shaving them all off with an obsessive's zeal, even the soft, downy ones on her back; they both knew all too well that hairs were absolute bastards when it came to peeling the latex off. He also knew she would have left a bare strip on the inside of the crack of her perfectly rounded ass; the first time they'd played with latex paint, she'd farted during sex and inflated a little balloon from her rear end, and that had been so funny it had rather spoiled the moment.

He'd known 'Chelle Tran for the best part of five years, four of those as his sometime live-in lover – she kept her apartment across town as it was closer than Guidry's estate for her office. She was of entrancing mixed race: half Vietnamese, half African American of Masai descent. She possessed dark, chocolate skin, long, slender legs, and a height that matched Guidry's six feet. She worked for the wealth management company that had handled the family fortune before Wildus had frittered through most of it, and they'd first met at his parent's funeral. Guidry and 'Chelle had connected almost immediately over the twin coffins of Mr. and Mrs. Thomas Guidry —, 'Chelle having commented upon how unfortunate it was that Guidry's parents were unable to have open caskets.

'Chelle was everything Guidry had ever fantasized about in a lover; she was an adventurous, exploratory kind of gal with a *try anything once* attitude and an incredibly dirty mind. Her opening gambit to Guidry – after the open casket remark – was she was actively bisexual and would love to fuck the female funeral home assistant whilst he fucked them both alternately in the ass.

As much as the dirty talk gave Guidry a hard-on that lasted all the way through his parent's funeral, the actual realization of 'Chelle's fantasy amongst the display coffins had topped the day off wonderfully.

So, there was that.

There was also the fact that if it hadn't been for 'Chelle's generous wage and that she was as mercenary with her client's money as she was with her own and always on the lookout for a deal or the next opportunity, or her unerring belief in him as an inventor, the Guidry pile would have been foreclosed at least two years ago. And, she looked good enough to rub his aching dick all over in her rubber get-up.

"I'll be up in a minute."

Guidry allowed his eyes the satisfaction of roaming over his woman's body; she'd painted the nails on her long, suckable toes a bright, wet red – just the thought of them around his cock made it twitch.

"You'd better be, lover…"

'Chelle put on her stern, schoolmarm voice. She waved the E-Stim wand, one of Guidry's more successful inventions, and a blue-white electric spark arced between its twin prongs. With her free-hand, 'Chelle parted her swollen, red-painted pussy lips to show him her dainty pink inner lips, which offered a delicious contrast to her dark-toned skin. Guidry saw that she was beyond wet, her pink flesh glistening in the harsh florescent basement lights. 'Chelle ran a long, slender finger the full length of her slit, lifted it to her whore-red gloss lips, and sucked off the moisture.

"I promise."

Guidry gave her his best, most reassuring smile, even though he'd already decided that he was going to give his time machine one more go, but this time, he was going to go with the thing.

'Chelle tipped him a wink, and headed back up the stairs, her vertiginous shoes *click-clacking* on the stone steps.

So, it was only three one-thousandths of a second back in time, hardly Marty McFly's thirty years, however, time travel *was* time travel . Besides, with his accurate data capture system, it was one-hundred percent provable, and Guidry knew full well that data like that was Nobel Prize material.

CHAPTER TWO

1.

uidry stared down at the time travel device he'd spent the past six months and change perfecting. Other than the fact he had homed its workings inside a sex toy, the thing appeared unremarkable. Outwardly, it was a simple black plastic cylinder that, indeed, did resemble a large flashlight upon which Guidry had added an LCD readout on one side and a hand-painted **#2** on its top surface. Of course, all the technology that enabled it to create the temporary wormhole through which the device slipped backward in time was contained inside, amidst a manic tangle of wires and microchips. There was a smaller box within the case, which Guidry considered the heart of the machine. It was soldered onto the motherboard next to the Bluetooth transmitter; it generated the temporal disrupter field that had made possible the unexceptional jump in time.

Guidry vacated his chair and stood a foot or so away from the device. The field the thing generated was a considerable one – at least fifteen feet, by his calculations – so he figured it was close enough. Guidry's fingers skated over his smart phone's screen as he brought up the app he'd created to remotely control his device.

Then he undressed. Guidry had seen enough science fiction movies to know one had to be naked to travel in time. He placed his clothes in a neat pile by his feet.

Guidry paused to savor the moment, finger poised over the unimaginatively labeled *'Go'* button on his phone.

This was it.

Wildus Guidry Esq. was about to become the first person in the whole history of forever to actually travel back in time. The poignancy of what he was about to do hit him hard: no matter the miniscule distance, his journey was to be an incredible one. Guidry also knew, with further modification, he *should* be able to get his device to venture farther afield than three one thousandths of a second.

Guidry was mentally writing his Time Magazine when he gingerly brushed his phone's screen.

The first thing he became aware of was a weird *pushing* sensation in his innards as if his gut were straining to get out through his skin. Even his dick twitched to attention and ached with a concrete hard-on, the likes of which he had not experienced since tenth grade. Then his vision blurred and everything turned milky white as the device created a time bubble around him.

And then there were sparks and flashes of bright white-blue light accompanied by a cacophony of shrill squeals that reminded Guidry of those strained, whale song farts 'Chelle made when she was trying to be discrete on the toilet.

Guidry's head throbbed, and his brain felt as if it would at any minute make a break for freedom out through his nose, ears, and eye sockets. He squeezed his eyes tight shut and pinched his nose with finger and thumb, genuinely concerned that his cerebral cortex would any minute begin its escape.

There was a jolt and an ear-piercing, tearing noise that seemed to come from *inside* Guidry's head

Then all was quiet.

Guidry opened his eyes and pinched his nose, relieved to learn that his brain – along with the rest of his internal organs – had stayed put during his jaunt through time.

He looked around and saw that the nebulous whiteness had dissipated. He was disappointed to see that his basement looked exactly the same as it did before, though; there was even the neat pile of clothes at his bare feet, which made him feel a little foolish.

Ever the scientist, Guidry checked the gauge on his device, and sure enough, he'd traveled precisely three one thousandths of a second back in time.

Elated, yet at the same time feeling deflated, by his achievement, Guidry comforted himself with the thought that if nothing else, he'd invented one hell of an – *acidless* – acid trip.

Yet, somehow – and Guidry did factor in the high possibility of this being nothing more than wishful thinking – it *felt* different. It was nothing he could quite lay a finger on, or even quantify scientifically, just something so subtle as to be hardly perceptible at all.

As Guidry's hearing returned from behind the incessant ringing the trip had created, he became aware of noise from beyond the basement door. It was the muffled *thud thud thud* of a repetitive baseline, and mostly indecipherable lyrics of hard-core rap: no doubt extolling the virtues of bitches, booty, and bullets. Guidry hated rap music; he thought it was just talentless black people shouting over perfectly good music. So, he was somewhat bemused as to why 'Chelle would have chosen it as the soundtrack to their evening's fucking.

Guidry decided it was his duty as a scientist – and the first person ever to have traveled in time – to explore the world of the past, even though he was mere fractions of a second behind. He would make the jump back to his own time in a while, even though it was probably unnecessary, he still had to test the device's ability to return – he knew his ordered brain would insist. *It would be foolish to fuck with that old stalwart of sci-fi, the space-time-continuum,* he thought, smiling at the fictional misnomer.

He glanced again at the LCD numbers on the device, confirmed that they had transmitted to his phone, and made ready to leave the basement.

He also made the decision to eschew redressing; it would be easy enough for Guidry to explain both his nude state and monster erection to 'Chelle considering the teaser she'd just given him. He knew that she would be waiting upstairs on their spacious play bed with its black, latex sheets, all wet and ready for him. And, with any luck she *had* started without him – there was nothing finer than finding his woman with her fist stuffed up the wrist in her sodden cunt, and her nipple between her teeth.

The cold concrete steps made Guidry shiver, and the soles of his feet quickly turned numb. He grimaced as the music grew louder with each step towards the basement door unless it was an integral part of whatever role-play scene, 'Chelle had dreamed up this time, Guidry was going to insist she turn it off before it killed his wood.

"Well, here goes nothing," Guidry said to thin air.

He let out a sigh and pulled open the basement door with a sharp tug and narrowly missed hitting his jutting prick with the handle. Guidry recoiled, suddenly all too conscious of his nakedness. He stood frozen to the spot with his mouth agape as both he and his erect penis stared through the doorway.

This was not his kitchen.

Hell, it was not even his house.

Guidry found himself confronted with what appeared to be a sex club where his kitchen should have been. It was complete with subdued lighting, trashy, easy-to-wipe-down furniture, and myriad naked copulating couples who adorned said furniture, the dance floor, and stools along the bar.

As the thumping music pounded through Guidry's chest, he noted through the dim light that the club appeared to contain an inordinate number of naked conjoined people, most of whom were engrossed in sweaty couplings with similarly afflicted pairings, 'single' people and in some cases, themselves. Also, some of the orgy's participants appeared to Guidry to be far too young to be nude and in a sex club.

Guidry shook his head as if to empty it out, but his mind raced ahead anyway. It would appear his miniscule time-jump had brought him to – where? An alternate universe? A whole new timeline, perhaps? His own universe, but within a bizarre fetish club in which patrons went to extraordinary lengths with their fancy dress on Siamese Twin Night?

Or, what if his device had killed him and he'd wound up in some odd afterlife?

"Are you coming in, or not?" a voice purred in his left ear, and long fingers coiled themselves around his dick.

Guidry twisted his head around and down, and saw the owner of the delightful fingers: a strikingly beautiful woman with mesmerizing blue eyes, spiked up, short black hair, and a sultry smile that showed perfect teeth through plump, red lips. Sitting on the chocolate-brown leather couch thigh-to-thigh with the woman was a broad-shouldered, muscular guy with a ruggedly handsome face topped by a bald, shiny head. He shared the same exotic mid-tan color skin tone with his woman, which Guidry could see had a subtle grayish tinge to it. The guy flashed a mischievous smile, and Guidry suddenly felt self-conscious that the guy's – wife, girlfriend, casual fuck? – had her hand around his penis.

The couple were totally and completely naked in keeping with all the other patrons in the club; even the bar staff appeared to be completely nude. The guy was completely hairless, his chest, arms, legs, and thick, jutting dick were all denuded. The woman, aside from her shock of hair, was similarly epilated. Even in the poor light, Guidry could see she had removed the fine downy hairs from her arms and back.

"I'm Kate," the woman introduced herself as she gently pulled Guidry into the club by his dick, "And this is Andrew."

She nodded toward her man as the door closed gently behind Guidry.

"No surname, I'm afraid, we find we're unique enough," she laughed pleasantly.

"Pleased to meet ya," Andrew said as he leaned over to shake hands.

"Likewise, I'm Wildus," Guidry shook hands with the man whose companion still had a firm hold of his prick.

It was at that point that Guidry noticed that the couple were literally joined at the hip. And the torso, as it happened – right up to their armpits: Andrew's left to Kate's right. Andrew's left arm was draped around his gal's shoulders like a teenager on a movie date, while Kate's right arm dangled to the front and nestled between the two, and was somewhat smaller than her left arm, which made it look underdeveloped. Guidry saw that there was a large knot of flesh almost the size of a cantaloupe on the shoulder blade that the two shared. From the lump, there bulged bony knobs that had the outline of fingers – like a tadpole about to burst through with its front legs – and Guidry was sure that it was moving.

"Why don't you join us?" Kate's words dripped suggestion.

Guidry looked down at her striking, upturned face. He couldn't help himself but cast his eyes down to admire her firm, fleshy tits and flat stomach, and then down again to the bare, fleshy mound of her sex. There, Guidry could just about make out the faint groove of the beginning of Kate's pussy slit.

"I guess, I should."

Guidry glanced down at Kate's hand that was now massaging his balls.

"Thank you!"

Kate pulled Guidry's genitals toward her face, and he felt her voluptuous lips close around the swollen bulb of his prick as it disappeared into her mouth.

Guidry groaned out his pleasure and instinctively gripped Kate's head with both hands to pull her onto his throbbing cock.

"That's the way," Andrew encouraged with a warm smile.

"Enjoy, *New Friend*."

Guidry felt his dick slide with ease down Kate's throat, where it stopped only when her teeth met its base. He stroked his hands over along the soft, smooth skin of Kate's neck and around to her throat. There he could feel the fat bulge of his dick whilst she masturbated him with her esophageal muscles.

While Kate fucked Guidry's dick with her throat, Andrew snaked an arm around his woman to finger his ass: Guidry peered out of the window above the strange couple's heads.

Where the neatly landscaped grounds of the Guidry family home should have been were now long, narrow streets soaking in the darkness of the late hour. Guidry could make out the familiar contours of his gardens in the ups and downs of the meandering cobbled streets, and there was even a glassy-surfaced duck pond beneath the town square's clock tower – right where his father's ornamental Koi pond had been back before he'd pressed the Go button.

The streets themselves were lined with sex shops, strip joints, and brothels – each one advertising its wares by means of neon signs that lit up the night with their gaudy glow. Guidry marveled at the window displays, none of which would have been allowed in any of the places he'd ever visited. The stores' windows were stacked high with plastic phalluses of every imaginable shape, size, and color, accompanied by realistic fake vaginas and disembodied sex doll heads in plastic-fronted boxes. The strip joints had real, live strippers in *their* displays, who danced and gyrated naked to entice customers the best they could in their confined spaces. The brothels plied their trade by showing their wares as a roadside grocer displays his: naked girls – and guys – were crowded into the window spaces on their backs, legs wide open, and epilated genitals on full display.

On the streets, Guidry could see people sauntering slowly, pausing to peruse the fleshy goods on display. As with everyone he'd seen so far, the pedestrians were completely naked, as if clothes were entirely unheard of there. Some of them had abandoned their perusals and were wantonly – and animatedly – fucking in store doorways or in the middle of the street. As with the copulating crowd in the club, the popular couplings seemed to comprise man-woman/woman-man conjoined twins. That way, each one could penetrate one of the opposite sex while writhing around within the unholy union.

And, to Guidry's utter astonishment, a large proportion of the population – behind the window displays, on the street, and in the club – appeared to be conjoined.

There were the expected combinations of two conjoined people, like Kate/Andrew. And, as with Guidry's current fellatrix and her mate, most were not identical twins, as should be the norm, given the biology behind conjoined twins. It was more the multiples of three, four – there was even a *five*-person amalgam, all joined at the chest and having an orgy with themselves in the center of the dance floor – that astounded Guidry, along with the seemingly random way in which they were joined together.

Some were joined by the head, others by their arms, legs, hips, or torso – still others by combinations of all four. There were those with heads and limbs sprouting from backs, chests, and bellies, and some with dicks and gaping cunts that emerged in seemingly random combinations from all conceivable places around their bodies. There was a guy joined at the face with his twin, who had a fully formed vulva in each armpit, and some with three, four, even six legs, which made them resemble odd, scuttling insects; still more had an entire half a person jutting out from their bodies, as if they were being absorbed.

Despite the wonderful sensations, Kate was conjuring within his dick, Guidry's head spun with question after question not least of which was – *just what the fuck is this place?*

Guidry knew for certain that he had jumped back in time – his ever so reliable sensors on the device had told him that much. But, the bizarreness of the place he'd found himself in couldn't possibly be explained in terms of time travel.

Could it?

"There'll be plenty of time for your questions later," Andrew said, as if reading Guidry's mind.

"First, you enjoy us."

Kate pulled her head back, and Guidry's dick slid out: its bulbous, purple end slick with mucus from deep down in her throat. She smiled up at Guidry; her scarlet lipstick smeared into slutty blurred edges around her mouth.

Kate/Andrew lay back on the couch. Kate spread wide her legs and used one of her hands, along with one of Andrew's, to pull apart the engorged flaps of her labia, and Guidry caught the cloying, meaty scent of her cunt. She pulled on each of her jutting her nipples in turn with her smaller hand to make them inflamed and angry-red.

Guidry knelt down between Kate's legs and aimed his dick at her glistening, fleshy hole, ignoring the multitude of tiny bumps that nestled around it. He eased himself down, fighting the urge to plunge straight into her hot vagina, eager to savor the exquisite touch of her on his most sensitive part – he was inside of her.

She let out a delicate *ahhhh* as Guidry slid deep inside her cunt and not stopping until the natural buffers of their pubic bones ground together. As Guidry began with long, slow thrusts into Kate, he was aware of Andrew's erection rubbing against his thigh, and the man's fingers slipping inside his anus.

They kissed as they fucked the three of them. Three tongues probed and wrestled, five hands caressed, probed, and invaded. Guidry found himself aroused to bursting point with Andrew's ever-present cock rubbing on his leg.

Kate came first. She climaxed with a loud shriek that attracted the attention of everyone in the club, even above the thrum of the music. Heads turned, sex halted, and there was even a small ripple of applause from the occupants of the other couches around the room. Andrew was next – his engorged dick blew its hot sticky cargo all over Guidry's leg. Some of the gooey spray spurted onto Guidry's face, and it tasted salty-sweet in the corner of his mouth. Kate licked the semen away as Guidry enjoyed his own orgasm and pumped his own come deep into her pussy.

Spent, more exhausted than he'd ever felt post-coital, Guidry slipped his dick out of Kate's pussy with a wet *slurp*. It was followed by a goodly amount of creamy white fluid, which Kate scooped up with one hand and sucked greedily from her fingers like those greasy-faced people on fried chicken commercials.

"I have to go," Guidry panted, suddenly aware of how long he'd been there.

Where?

"No worries, buddy."

Andrew slapped him on the shoulder.

"None at all," Kate smiled, her mouth gummy with strings of Guidry's jizz.

"We hope to see you again soon."

"You will, most definitely."

Guidry had used the line a million times before in his philandering past, but realized he actually meant it. After all, he still had countless questions and innumerable things to straighten out in his head, but 'Chelle was waiting for him – he had to get back to the time he'd come from.

Guidry climbed off of the couch. His dick, dripping wet down to his balls, was still rock hard and pointing at Kate's spread pussy like a kid picking out its favorite thing in the toy store. As he stepped back toward the door, Kate/Andrew were busy snowballing his semen between their hungry mouths. Andrew had four fingers al the way to the knuckles in Kate's vagina, and she was tugging on her attached mate's ramrod prick. Guidry doubted very much they were going to miss him.

2.

The trip back to his own time was less of a shock to Guidry's system, save for the bright flashes that hurt his eyes, which had had grown accustomed to the lighting in the dingy sex club. He stood for a second or two, relishing the quietness of the basement that looked exactly the same as it had just (*literally*!) moments before when it had led up to the outlandish club. Only, it *felt* different, and that worried him.

The readout on the time travel device informed Guidry that he was, indeed, back to where he started. But, being a novice in the whole business of time travel, he was unsure as to whether or not the half-hour or so he'd spent fucking Kate/Andrew would have passed here as well. And, if 'Chelle had been left waiting for him in an unrequited state of arousal; if so, he knew he'd be in for a rough time of it when he showed his face in their playroom.

As it turned out, Guidry needn't have worried.

Still naked, he'd raced from the basement and upstairs to the bedroom – with a pit-stop at the bathroom to wipe down his sweaty body with a towel – to find 'Chelle reclined on the bed, resplendent in her painted-on body suit with her fingers idly fiddling with her clit.

"Hey, lover," 'Chelle gave Guidry her most lascivious smile.

"I was just getting warmed up here."

She flicked her engorged clitoris with a scarlet, claw-like fingernail, and gasped as its pleasures shuddered through her.

Guidry breathed a sigh of relief; the device had deposited him back at the exact moment he'd hit the Go button. So, to his girlfriend, it was as if he'd never been gone at all. In fact, Guidry had made it to their boudoir so quick that the porn movie 'Chelle had selected was only just beginning and was still on the wholly unnecessary preamble scene in which an improbably dressed – and easily over eighteen – schoolgirl was bending over her desk to show the teacher she was wearing tiny pink panties.

"You stink of come."

'Chelle inhaled deeply and gave a throaty moan as Guidry climbed on to the bed.

"You diffused the bomb for me, darling. Thank you." she purred.

Often, when faced with the prospect of a lengthy sex session with 'Chelle, Guidry would masturbate beforehand to maintain his stamina. In their early days together, he'd discovered that the sensual combination of 'Chelle's tighter-than-tight pussy, never-say-no attitude to anything, and everything of a sexual nature would often result in premature ejaculation and a grim hangover of disappointment. Sometimes, 'Chelle would take him in hand, as it were, but more often, Guidry would prefer to do it – he rather enjoyed the self-indulgence.

And yet tonight, no matter how damned sexy 'Chelle looked, covered ankles to throat in shiny latex, or how eagerly she sucked his balls into her mouth, ground her sopping wet cunt onto his face 'till she orgasmed and filled his nostrils with her juices, or pinched his nipples so hard he squealed out loud, Guidry just couldn't get his dick to play ball.

As for 'Chelle, with a disappointed look etched all over her face, she attempted to thumb his soft penis into her rapidly drying vagina.

Guidry decided to call it a night; 'Chelle left his house without peeling off the latex, a humiliated air about her, and tears in her eyes.

Of course, Guidry had been chivalrous and told 'Chelle it wasn't her; it was *him*, which was mostly true. It wasn't so much he'd fucked Kate/Andrew just moments before, as he still enjoyed the reset rate of a fifteen-year-old – his mind was still back in the strange place. There, it raced with the enigma his experiment had presented and the uncountable questions thus posed. That, and delightful memories of the uninhibited naked, conjoined people and all of the sexual delights that they had to offer.

Wildus Guidry just couldn't wait to go back.

CHAPTER THREE: *0.0026*

1.

"Imagine time as one of those old-time slide projectors," Andrew explained to Guidry, his voice raised above the booming noise in the club, "the kind with the carousel everyone had before everything got all electronic and *PowerPoint*."

"I'm not following you," Guidry shouted. He was straining to hear above the intrusive, heavy beat, and his concentration was marred somewhat by the expert blowjob he was receiving from Kate.

Andrew raised his voice still higher and gave Guidry a patient smile.

"Time exists in slices – each one like a slide in the carousel," he explained. "Only, now there are only the two slides left – this one, and yours."

"Which means?" Guidry squirmed in his seat as Kate's tongue probed down the sensitive eye of his penis.

"Which means this is as far back in time as you can go," Andrew explained with a grin. "It really is no big deal when you consider the fact that time is an abstract concept anyway

– created to mark the passage of human life. It's a fact most people seem to forget when theorizing about time travel. A bit like developing theories about the tooth fairy, I guess."

Guidry nodded as if he understood. Truth was, he was still struggling to take all of it in, what with this being only his second trip back in time. Hell, he wasn't even sure how much of Kate/Andrew's time had elapsed since his last visit. It had been less than twenty-four hours in his own timeframe, but the lump on his new friend's back had grown considerably since their previous encounter. It was now the size of a newborn baby, and the shapes of its limbs beneath the taut skin were even more defined.

And - was that the outline of a face?

"You seem to know a lot about time travel," Guidry said. "Are you a physicist?"

"No, no, no. Far from it," Andrew laughed. "Everyone here knows about time travel – we learn about it in school. Many, many years ago, we had the means to go back to a whole variety of times."

His eyes saddened.

"But that was before Number One was destroyed and put an end to all of that."

"Number One?"

Guidry's mind flitted away from the delightful suction of Kate's mouth on his dick.

"It's what they called the Time Gadget back in the day." Andrew was forced to shout as the DJ changed music tracks and the din grew inexplicably louder.

"My first prototype," Guidry thought out loud.

"What's that?" Andrew cupped his free hand to his ear.

"I said, I want you to tell me everything."

"Everything?" Andrew looked at him, puzzled. "How much time have you got?"

Guidry looked at Andrew with a puzzled expression, as if trying to figure out a particularly difficult conundrum. "*Err*, well… all of it, I guess," he replied.

"Then I suggest that we go back to our place," Andrew mouthed and pointed to the club's exit. "It'll be quieter." He gave Kate a tug, and she relinquished Guidry's dick before he'd had the chance to come. It bounced from her mouth like a loosened spring and stood to attention, glistening wet from her saliva.

"If we're going outside, you'd best take off your clothes." Kate winked at Guidry.

"She's right," Andrew added, "we need to make sure you fit in."

Even stark naked, Guidry didn't feel much like he fitted in. Among the patrons in the sex club and the people walking the darkening streets outside, he stood out as one of only a few *singles*. Almost everyone else was conjoined, in some way or another, or sported the random, bulbous lumps that appeared commonplace. There was also the matter of his smattering of dark body hair, which Kate/Andrew suggested he do something about before his next visit.

The streets beyond the club hummed with the faint buzz of innumerable neon signs and had a pervading stink of sex about them; it clung to the garish red brick in a piscine haze, an earthy, meaty odor that reminded Guidry of whorehouse pussy and old, semen-filled condoms. Glancing over his shoulder at the tawdry facade of the sex club, *Action 24/7*, and reminded himself the row of aging buildings in which it stood was precisely where his house was standing in another timeline.

Soon, Guidry found himself in Kate/Andrew's apartment, sipping from a large glass of iced tea (unsweetened) that had thick lemon wedges bobbing about in it beneath the fat ice cubes, as if desperate to take a gasp of air.

"We used to believe that the other timelines we visited were parallel universes," Andrew continued. "But now we know that they are just other slides in time's great carousel." He smiled, as if pleased with his poetic simile.

"You said this time and mine were the only ones left, what happened to the others?" Guidry quizzed.

Andrew stared at him, eyes wide like a rabbit caught in headlights.

Kate broke into the conversation, "It's quite fortuitous that we reproduce asexually." She twisted her body around to show Guidry the hefty, squirming lump on the scapula she and Andrew shared. She received what Guidry interpreted as a grateful smile from her partner and continued. "People in your time thought our pioneers were Siamese twins," She giggled.

"Siamese twins are *your* people?"

"Not all of them," Kate replied. "Conjoined embryos are a genuine phenomenon with your people – like Chang and Eng Bunker – they are the result of an unsuccessfully split embryo. Our DNA recombination and cell mutations occur during mitosis; hence, we experience *asexual* reproduction." She winked once more at Guidry. "But, some Siamese twins in your time were our early adventurers, bravely exploring the alternate timelines."

"They discovered the timelines eventually catch up with each other," Andrew joined in. "And when they do, one takes over the other."

"Takes over?" Guidry couldn't hide the alarm in his voice.

"Don't panic, friend," Andrew laughed as he and Kate maneuvered themselves so Kate was sitting astride Guidry, her gaping vagina a moist, dark hole above his prick. "By our calculations, based on the *Catch-Up Rate –*"

"– which is a constant," Kate interrupted, at the same time rubbing her stiff nipples in Guidry's face.

"Thank you, Kate." Andrew snorted his annoyance. "Unless something catastrophic is done to accelerate the Rate, it's going to be over two hundred thousand years before our respective lines occupy the same time; a hell of a long time after any of us have ceased giving a shit!"

The three laughed together.

"So, if you guys reproduce like – this." Guidry pointed at the shifting lump on Kate/Andrew's back. "What's with all the fucking?"

"For *fun*," Kate giggled as Andrew grasped Guidry's twitching dick and guided it up into her asshole.

"And it's how we feed," Andrew continued.

"We exchange energy through penetrative sex."

"You have to fuck to live?" Guidry gasped; Kate's anus felt exceptionally tight around his cock.

"Same reason sharks have to keep on swimming." Andrew nodded and slid his hand between Kate and Guidry to wriggle three fingers into Kate's vagina.

"It doesn't matter what we do, or where it goes, it's the *penetration* that counts," Kate panted as she rocked her body to and fro to massage Guidry with her insides.

Guidry's questions began to leak out of his brain as waves of ecstasy flooded its synapses with sex-induced endorphins. He felt every millimeter of his prick flesh against the hot, slick walls of Kate's rectum, and the rough grating of her next bowel movement against his tip. And that, along with the wiggling motion of Andrew's fingers in Kate's cunt, Guidry's head emptied – along with his balls.

As he came, Guidry's hand strayed to the lump on Kate/Andrew's back. His fingers touched a warm, sticky slime oozing from the lump and ragged edges of what felt like ripped flesh and fingers – he felt *fingers*.

2.

Back in his basement, back in his own time, Guidry stared down at his slack dick as he waited for his post-time travel head to quit spinning. He mused over the brown streaks of dried shit and semen that decorated his shaft and relived fond thoughts of Kate's wonderfully tight asshole that had literally strangled the orgasm out of him.

Guidry tussled with his conflicting emotions: elation at having traveled back in time – he was still half-convinced what he had discovered was some kind of parallel reality and that Kate/Andrew's people had got their theories wrong – and bitter disappointment at having learned that was as far back as time travel could ever go.

Big fucking deal.

Who in God's name would be interested in traveling back fractions of a second to see weird, sex-obsessed, conjoined people who fucked to eat and reproduced via ugly buds? Oh yeah, he'd decided to give the people the epithet *Buds* as it seemed most appropriate since they hadn't awarded themselves a collective noun – who in God's name doesn't have a fucking collective noun? – and they reproduced like some kind of obscene sea creatures.

People interested in time travel wanted to see ancient civilizations, Jesus, and fucking dinosaurs!

Guidry sighed and pulled his pants back on, although he wasn't sure as to why the house was empty. He'd ignored 'Chelle's heavy hints at a night in *to play* in favor of another jaunt, to visit his new friends and learn more about their bizarre world, even though he knew she'd be terribly pissed.

Weary, Guidry made his way out of the basement, very much focused on hitting the sack and staying there until at least lunchtime the following day. As he stepped over Device #2, his tired eyes barely registered its readout had changed once again.

CHAPTER FOUR: *0.0021*

"You haven't called me in over a week!"

'Chelle was furious with him. Guidry could tell by the way her nostrils flared and little flecks of spittle flew from her lips as she shouted.

"And just what the fuck is this all about!?" she ranted.

Guidry looked down at his naked, epilated body; he felt like a small child caught with his hand in the candy jar. His timid, shriveled penis and ball sack illustrated both his shame and the cold air in the basement.

"I – I was going to call you," Guidry lied.

"I've been very busy."

"I can fucking see how busy you've been, Wildus," 'Chelle snarled at him. "Playing with your dumb little fuck toy!" She poked a bare toe at the device that sat quietly by

Guidry's feet. She regretted buying him the motherfucking *Fucklight* now; it was supposed to have been an enhancement to their fucking, not a *replacement*. And what was with the readouts?

"It's not a sex toy, 'Chelle – not anymore," Guidry tried to explain, although he figured it an obvious conclusion for her to jump to.

He *was* standing in his basement, just about to hit the *Go* button on his cell phone, and he was as naked as the day he was born in front of the thing. Added to that, his dick had been semi-tumescent in anticipation of another visit with Kate/Andrew before 'Chelle had stormed in and started yelling.

And, since when did his girlfriend have a goddamned key to the house?

'Chelle had herself a spare key cut early on in their relationship; she'd made an impression of it on a wax block, and she knew a guy for such occasions. She'd pulled the stunt before with other men and on many an instance had caught them *in flagrante delicto* when they'd stopped calling her – her suspicions having once again been proven correct. One guy, she'd caught fucking his Pyrenean Mountain dog when she'd let herself into his apartment, and he'd even had the audacity to get nasty with *her* when she'd refused to make it a three-way!

She'd noticed a change in Guidry's behavior a couple of weeks ago, around the time he'd begun shaving off his body hair. Sure, they both kept their genitals smooth, as there was nothing finer than the feel of bare skin on bare skin – especially when lubricated with copious amounts of her pussy juice – but this turn of events had seemed slightly odd, even for Guidry.

Then, shortly before he'd quit calling her, 'Chelle had noticed Guidry would slip out of bed before she'd had the chance to get her hands, (or mouth, cunt, or ass) around his dick to *'go pee.'* There had been a time – not all that long ago – that if Guidry had a full bladder before sex, he'd micturate in 'Chelle's willing mouth, and she'd gulp it down like it was an expensive dessert wine.

But, even more peculiar was Guidry would return to bed mere moments later stinking of come and with what looked – and felt – like day-old stubble on his chin and around his dick, despite having been smooth as a baby's proverbial when they'd climbed in to bed.

Confused, 'Chelle had said nothing. The truth was, she was not sure *what* to say, even when Guidry's attempts to fuck her was, to say the least, lackluster. He'd try his damndest to satisfy her, of course, his dick never more than half-mast and more often than not eating her out to the tune of two – sometimes three – orgasms in a session. At least she had that pleasure for her troubles; Guidry had always been good with that long, lithe tongue of his, even if his chin was abrasive against the soft skin of her thighs – she had a tendency to break out in a horrendous rash afterward.

What 'Chelle couldn't figure out – apart from the rapid stubble growth, the answer to that conundrum would allude her until she discovered Guidry's secret – was *why in fuck's name was her boyfriend so obviously sneaking to the bathroom to jerk off?* She was a more than willing fuck partner, who had never said *no* to anything he'd asked – even when it came to covering herself head-to-toe in white makeup and laying stock-still, pretending to be a corpse while he fucked her asshole. Also, 'Chelle had contemplated, if that *was* what he was up to, then Guidry had become the world's fucking fastest masturbator!

After so long, he'd just quit inviting her over for dinner and cock, and 'Chelle assumed he'd gotten himself absorbed in another one of his crazy inventions. Guidry tended toward the obsessive when he was working on something new – never once had she questioned his fidelity. He'd done this to her before, so she wasn't overly concerned, but once it had gotten to seven days without so much as an SMS, 'Chelle had decided to break out that spare key.

She found herself halfway down the stairs of Guidry's chilly basement with the intention of seducing him away from his work. She'd squeezed her statuesque frame into one of his favorites, a metallic blue mini dress with a down-to-the-navel cowl neck that exposed her tits as its flimsy fabric swung around her neck. She was barefoot, as was her lover's preference, and had inserted an impressive string of twelve giant anal beads, which jostled and clacked together inside the farthest recesses of her bowels each time she moved.

'Chelle looked down on the awkwardly naked Guidry and thought just how much he looked like a little boy who was ashamed of her for the slick wetness that spread between her legs. 'Chelle pursed her lips at him and let the silence do her talking.

"It's – it's a time machine." Guidry never could beat *The Silence*. 'Chelle was a grandmaster at its use – or *abuse* – to be more precise, and he was always the one to break it and therefore lose. "Or, at least that's what it's supposed to be." He glanced down at the inert thing at his feet at the gauge that read 0.0021.

"A time machine." 'Chelle pulled a pouty face to go along with the incredulity in her tone.

"You're fucking kidding me?" She took a step back from the device; the glass beads in her rectum chinked together and made a noise like wind chimes.

Guidry shook his head. "I promise you, I'm not…" he said. A feeling of relief swept over him, and Guidry realized just how good it felt to have someone on his timeline to talk to about his discovery.

"You'd better not be fucking with me, Wildus." 'Chelle gave him her hard-bitch stare. "Or with anyone else, for that matter." She glanced around, as if looking for someplace he could have secreted another woman.

"I promise you, there's no one else here," Guidry told her, which was not entirely a lie since his new fuck buddies were not actually *there*. "I've been working on the time machine all along. I'm sorry if I neglected you – *us*."

Again, the Great 'Chelle Silence.

"Only, I'm not entirely sure what it is I've discovered." Guidry fell for his girlfriend's ruse a second time.

'Chelle folded her arms beneath her bust; her left breast popped out of the silky material of her dress, its nipple soft, flat, and begging to be clamped.

"So," 'Chelle growled, "tell me."

Guidry did his best to explain about how the device had transported him mere fractions of a second back in time, but how different things were back there. He left out the part about the decreasing number on his device's display, as he wasn't entirely certain of its significance and it left an uneasy niggle at the back of his mind – like an infuriating itch he just couldn't reach.

He also told 'Chelle about the dark, dank streets that stank of sex and the plethora of sex stores, clubs, and brothels. He regaled her with tales of the strange people that populated the other time – the *Buds* – and how they reproduced by fission and used sex merely for sustenance and recreation. He did omit the fact he'd kind of gotten into the habit of visiting on a daily basis, for days, weeks, of the Bud's time, only to return at the exact moment of departure, and it was as if he'd never been gone at all.

All the while, 'Chelle listened to Guidry with intent. She furrowed her brow as he spoke, and her shapely, brown tit rose and fell with the rhythm of her breath, its nipple puckered and stiff in the cool air. And, when he'd finished, 'Chelle just looked at him as if he'd just served her up the biggest heap of steaming bullcrap ever to have assaulted her ears.

"So," she said. "Show me."

"What?" Guidry looked worried.

"I said, show me." She uncrossed her arms and tucked her errant mammary back behind the slinky cowl. "Take me to your other place."

"Time," Guidry corrected.

"Now is not the time to get fucking pedantic, Wildus," 'Chelle snapped. "Take me now, or I'm fucking walking."

Guidry considered rising to the double *entendre,* but thought better of it, given 'Chelle's obvious confrontational mood.

"Okay, babe," Guidry sighed. "But you may want to undress first."

"What?" 'Chelle barked. "Do you really think I'm *that* fucking stupid?"

"It's not what you think." Guidry smiled for the first time since she'd stormed in. "Trust me!"

CHAPTER FIVE: 0.0017

'Chelle Tran saw straight away how come Guidry had suggested she undress before he'd activated his odd little device (she had also made a mental note to chastise him about ruining the ridiculously expensive *Fucklight* she'd bought him). The hot, dingy club he'd brought her to heaved with cavorting, sweating, and ever so nude people – many of whom, she noticed, were inexplicably conjoined exactly as Guidry had described. The music in the club was all but drowned out by the sounds of fornication, and the place had the lascivious air of the most depraved sex clubs she and Guidry had enjoyed back in their own time. It had the unmistakable, cloying stink of perspiration, pheromones, semen, and raw cunt hanging so thick in the air one could practically *see* it.

Always confident – and *thrilled* – to be naked, 'Chelle stood on the threshold of the club and let her bare skin absorb the wanton hedonism that greeted her. She had gone along with Guidry's instance that she undress thinking it merely a ruse to indoctrinate her into some bizarre new sexual game. It hadn't taken her too long, of course – she'd slipped out of the metallic dress in no time at all, and she hadn't been wearing any underwear. Guidry had insisted she keep the anal beads in.

From across the room, an odd-looking couple, who 'Chelle could see were joined pretty much the entire length of their bodies were waving them over with a smile on both their faces that implied familiarity. 'Chelle gave Guidry a hard look; they clearly had much to discuss upon their return.

Guidry grabbed hold of 'Chelle's hand and guided her with an expert's ease through the crowd. 'Chelle's eyes were everywhere as she stared in disbelief at the unlikely combinations of revelers around her.

There were couples, threesomes, foursomes, and moresomes, people with more arms and legs they ought to have had, some with two or more heads, some with one head and two bodies, males and females with jutting, glistening genitalia positioned about their bodies, and those with what appeared to be children sprouting from random places about their naked person. 'Chelle noted the strange people were all variations of the same skin color, considerably lighter than hers, and of a hue that reminded her of the brownish-gray of a child's mixed palette.

And as she gawked at the impossible spectacle surrounding her, 'Chelle began to wonder if Guidry hadn't somehow hypnotized her with his infernal machine – and this was all just some illusion he'd planted in her brain for his own nefarious means.

On more than one occasion, on their trek through the club, 'Chelle felt hands, moist erections, and slick, dripping vaginas caress her moistened skin. Mouths sucked and nibbled at her flesh, and tongues lapped at her salty sweat as she walked past the dense throng. On occasion, her sweat-dampened hand would slip from Guidry's, and twice, she found herself attempting to maneuver between a couple with a polite *pardon me,* only to find her passage blocked by a thick bridge of flesh that joined the pair.

Guidry tugged on 'Chelle's hand as he led her through the cavorting Buds, her glass beads playing a *click clack click* tattoo in her rectum as she wove in and out of the heaving, bodies. Through the club's windows, 'Chelle made out the neon-lit streets with their gaudy lights and shamelessly fornicating people, who mirrored perfectly the debauchery going on inside the club.

Although Guidry had told her almost everything he'd learned about the Buds, 'Chelle wasn't fully prepared for seeing them up so close and personal. So, she shuddered visibly when Kate/Andrew told her *hi* and offered hands for her to shake.

"I'm sorry," 'Chelle mumbled as she gingerly took Kate/Andrew's hand. "This is all very –"

"– don't mention it!" Kate sounded cheery above the cacophony of groans and slapping, clammy flesh. "I'm Kate, this is Andrew, and this is Mhari." Kate/Andrew spun around to reveal the young half-girl that sprouted from their shoulder blade.

"Hi," Mhari grinned.

'Chelle was taken aback, to say the least. Mhari had the appearance of a regular teenaged girl, except she was growing out of Kate/Andrew's back and only seemed to exist from just below her perky, jutting breasts, which came complete with large, puffy nipples. She boasted the same luscious, red hair as her mother and a pretty, cheerful face bestowed with the most delectable rosebud lips 'Chelle had ever seen.

Kate/Andrew's daughter also had a pair of perfectly formed arms, and there was what 'Chelle assumed to be the girl's leg sprouting from Andrew's right buttock. A large, bulbous bud grew from Andrew's ass crack, which bulged with the faint outline of what appeared to be toes; 'Chelle guessed it to be Mhari's other leg. 'Chelle took it all in, in glorious close up, and figured out for herself why Guidry had christened these people as he had.

"It's so good to finally meet you, 'Chelle." Kate grinned as she/Andrew spun back around to leave Mhari staring goggle-eyed at the orgy that ran rampant on the dance floor. "Wildus has told us so much about you."

"And he's told me absolutely nothing about you." 'Chelle gave a sardonic curl of the lip.

"Well, what would you like to know?" Andrew, ever cheery, asked her.

"Everything."

So, Kate/Andrew patiently went through their entire repertoire for 'Chelle's benefit, happy to leave Guidry and Mhari to take in the free live sex show. And, when they'd finished telling her everything there was to tell, 'Chelle simply stood in contemplative silence and struggled to process the gamut of outlandish information she'd just soaked up.

"Are you okay, babe?" Guidry slipped an arm around 'Chelle's waist. He found her skin to be sodden with slick sweat, which could either have been from the syrupy club atmosphere or her inwardly freaking out.

'Chelle nodded. "This is awesome, Wildus. No... This is *freakin'* awesome! These people literally *live* for this depraved, recreational sex. And *you* invented a way to get here." She absently stroked at her breast as she spoke; a fingernail hooked one jutting nipple.

"*Wow,*" she breathed.

There was a commotion on the dance floor, and the heaving sea of naked flesh parted. 'Chelle, Guidry, and Kate/Andrew/Mhari turned to look and saw the cavorting had ceased and all attention was on a conjoined couple in the center of the floor; their wet skin twinkled gaily in the multicolored disco lights that danced from above them. A man and a woman, the couple were melded together breastbone to breastbone with the lady's substantial tits flattened tight against her partner's chest. Their genitals were squeezed together, as if the two were permanently fucking, and they were both covered head-to-toe in irregular lumps of all shapes and sizes – from hen's egg to marrow. They appeared to be in considerable pain as they pushed against each other, as if each one was attempting to force their partner away.

"Oh, goody! It's a Separation," Kate declared with glee. "I do *love* Separations, they are *sooo* fucking sexy!" She giggled and playfully batted Andrew's dick with her hand so that it bobbed up and down like some denuded waterfowl.

Before 'Chelle or Guidry could ask the obvious, dumb question, there came a sickening sound, much like the rending of cheap cloth, and the dance floor couple separated and toppled over backward in opposite directions.

As much as 'Chelle wanted to look away, she found she couldn't. She clamped a hand to her mouth as her lunch made an impromptu dart for freedom, and she stared, mesmerized at the scene before her.

The conjoined couple had actually ripped themselves apart and were now no longer conjoined, and 'Chelle couldn't help but wonder who out of the pair the Bud had been, and who had been the *Bud-ee*. Where they had been joined was a gaping, jagged hole in their skin, through which the hard, white bone of both of their sternums and ribs shone. From the torn flesh flowed an oozing slop that drenched the couple's bellies and thighs, and painted them a steaming red/green color. The steaming odor of the slop wafted over to 'Chelle on the thick air; it stank of innards, spoiled meat, and excrement, like a dead man's fart.

As if that were not horror enough for 'Chelle's assaulted senses, the grotesque, naked crowd closed in on the newly divided Buds with aroused delight to poke fingers, toes, and cocks into the gaping wounds. Some ventured further and lapped at the viscous goo; collecting it with eager hands to smear over faces, breasts, and genitals. 'Chelle saw many of the deviant crowd were masturbating – themselves and each other – with the slimy gore, as if it were the world's finest, most erotic lubricant.

As she watched, the split couple struggled to their feet and acknowledged their audience. The woman took little time in impaling herself on the fat fist of an enormous guy, who was part of a conjoined three-way with a skinny guy and an elderly woman. The split guy was busy sticking his dick, to the hilt, down the throat of an attractive young girl Bud, who sprouted from the gaping vagina of a skeletally thin woman. She, in turn, was joined at the top of her head to a squat, fat guy's bald pate.

'Chelle watched the couple's Separation wounds heal with a preternatural rapidity: muscle had already covered the once-exposed bone, and the skin was knitting together either side of the Separation laceration to form a thin, raised white scar.

The sexual frenzy the couple's Separation had provoked spread throughout the club like wildfire. The horde of Buds in every imaginable array of combinations threw themselves into erotic encounters with everyone and anyone within reach. Hard, angry dicks found their way into wet, willing vaginas, assholes, and mouths; whilst other holes were stuffed to capacity with tongues, fingers, fists, and feet. Bodies slipped and slid against each other as the entire dance floor orgy became marinated in their juices, along with the slime from the freshly sundered Bud couple; the raw-steak stink of rot and body fluids choked the place.

'Chelle shocked herself upon discovering that she was fingering her pussy whilst watching the orgiastic shenanigans. She was also taken aback to see that, right by her side, Guidry was ensconced in the middle of a three-Bud combination – two-gals, one guy – fucking one of the women, who was tongue-wrestling the woman attached to her thigh. The guy in the combination had his cock buried to the hilt in Guidry's ass, and Guidry was taking it like an pro.

'Chelle was, fleetingly, disgusted at the thought that her man had most probably done this before with these people, most likely many times. But then, she thought to herself, wouldn't she have done exactly the same, given the circumstance?

Then, 'Chelle's attention was taken away from her philandering boyfriend as Kate's fingers joined hers deep inside her cunt. Startled at first – it was customary to ask before finger-fucking a person where she came from – her reticence melted in an instant as an expert thumb pressed firmly on her clit. 'Chelle found herself drawn into Kate/Andrew/Mhari's arms to be enveloped by their perspiring flesh.

Kate/Andrew/Mhari's middle arm groped openly at 'Chelle's breasts, kneading the pliant flesh and plucking at her nipples so deliciously hard she almost came on the spot. With astounding dexterity, Kate continued the thumb pressure on 'Chelle's swollen clitoris, massaged her G-spot with three fingers, and wriggled her pinkie finger into 'Chelle's puckered ass, where it tugged delightfully at the string attached to the beads that moved around inside her with an almost fluid motion. Andrew buried his hand in 'Chelle's hair to pull her to him for a long, deep kiss, and filled her mouth with his thick tongue.

It felt like heaven.

Sure, she'd had threesomes and orgies many times before, but this so very much different; there was something so erotically charged with her partners all being the *same* flesh, all part of the same body. 'Chelle felt as if her body was burning with flames of a pure orgasm, the likes of which she had never before experienced in her life; a force pulsing through to the very core of her being, while at the same time draining her energies out through her sex. All at the same time, 'Chelle felt she could fuck until her cunt was raw and bleeding, scale the highest rooftops, run forever, and sleep for an eternity.

In fact, she'd never felt so alive and sexually charged since the time she and her ex-husband had paid for time with a tantric sex hooker.

As 'Chelle allowed herself to be seduced into her parent's pleasures, Mhari strained to watch over their shoulder like an inquisitive teenager, her eyes wide with curiosity and arousal. And, to 'Chelle's surprise – and horror – she found that to be the biggest turn-on of the entire experience.

Overwhelmed by the sights, sounds, and smells of the sea of copulating bodies and the pleasures being served upon her, 'Chelle pulled away. As she did so, Kate's fingers slipped from inside her constricting pussy and a thick string of her juices snaked down her inner thigh.

'Chelle poked at Guidry to get his attention away from fucking and *being fucked*.

"Wildus…" 'Chelle said. "I have an idea."

THERE'S A SECOND PART TO THIS STORY

CHAPTER SIX: 0.0009

'Chelle's brothel idea was a resounding success; of that there could be no doubt whatsoever. In the six months since her revelation at the Bud's sex club, Guidry's house no longer had the threat of foreclosure hanging over it. As a matter of happenstance, William Henke, the bank's manager, was one of their most loyal clients, and thanks to him, much of the redecoration had been completed, and most of the place had been rewired.

Guidry had revisited the timeline 'Chelle had christened *Budworld* (simply because the people there didn't seem to have a name for it - to much consternation and argument from Guidry; he said the name sounded like some second-rate Michael Crichton novel) a dozen or so times since that first joint visit. And, on each occasion, 'Chelle had him bring back one of the Buds for the whorehouse she'd set up in Guidry's expansive ancestral home.

They'd started their peculiar harem with Kate/Andrew/Mhari under 'Chelle's strict instructions; Guidry had populated the place with the widest variety of Buds he could find, all of whom appeared most delighted with the arrangement.

The Buds appeared to be a sweet, naive race, who were more than thrilled with the endless rounds of depraved sex with humans *(did they never get tired?!)* and for the opportunity to live somewhere new and exciting. Having said that, they never actually left the confines of the house, which led Guidry to wonder just what they were getting from the arrangement.

As it happened, Guidry had been having niggling doubts over his continuing abuse of the time device. Not only was he certain he could hear his long-passed ancestors spinning in their graves at the desecration of their home, but he had a growing concern over the rapidly reducing number on the device's readout. With each trip, Guidry had noted the number dropped by a few ten thousandths of a second; more so when he traveled with the Buds. To his increasingly paranoid self, it felt like a countdown to something unpredictably unpleasant – possibly even *catastrophic*. And it was precisely why he was so vehemently opposed to 'Chelle's Budworld Vacation Plan scheme.

"Do I *have* to remind you, Wildus?" 'Chelle's lecturing tone brought him back to the present with a jolt. "That our high-end clients paying for sex vacations to Budworld have paid off your tax bill *and* contributed to most of the restoration of *your* house." She glowered at him from across the huge oak desk, which she'd had especially shipped in from Europe.

Guidry looked around at her newly renovated office, which had once been his father's study. 'Chelle had all of the old stuff ripped out and replaced with expensive, antique furniture which, to Guidry, looked pretty much the same as the original stuff.

"I do understand that, 'Chelle." Guidry was ashamed at just how meek he sounded – since when was he the fucking *submissive* in this relationship? "But the gap between the two timelines is getting shorter with each trip and –"

"– and *nothing*, Wildus!" 'Chelle cut him off rudely. "It's just fuckin' numbers. Nothing's actually happened, has it?"

"No," Guidry was forced to concede. "Not *yet*."

"Then that's a bridge we can cross if and when we have to," 'Chelle told him; the tone in her voice let him know the subject was now closed. She leaned back in her plush leather chair and smoothed her Gucci jacket over her breasts.

Guidry took the hint and let the subject drop. He also decided it was probably not the best time to go ahead with his plan to mention the discovery on the underside of his penis of a cluster of small warts that oozed sickly green pus that stank like death.

Or how, in the right light, the warts appeared to have teeny, tiny faces.

There was no doubting 'Chelle's business savvy. Coupled with her enviable network of disgustingly rich contacts, she had exploited the opportunity presented by Guidry's discovery and the Buds in the most profitable way possible. The Bud brothel had quickly become popular amongst 'Chelle's wealthiest, most discerning clients, and she had created a network of word-of-mouth, by-invitation-only clientele: the types who knew how to operate under the radar, and to whom discretion was a byword. Each and every one of 'Chelle Tran's customers knew how to keep a secret, especially a dirty, depraved one such as hers.

And they kept coming back for more, despite the fact that word spread amongst the clientele that a visit to

'Chelle's whorehouse of freaks would often leave patrons not only sexually satisfied beyond their wildest, sickest fantasies, but physically exhausted – as if they'd run a half marathon *and* gone twelve rounds with Mayweather.

Somehow, that heady combination (some clients had to be *carried* out!) meant repeat custom was never better.

It was the very nature of the Buds – with their multiple, infinitely varied, changing bodies – that appealed to those who preferred their sex strictly non-vanilla and with a definite twist of the bizarre. 'Chelle's house of ill-repute offered threesomes, foursomes, moresomes, and combinations of lovers that often defied all imagination. It brought in the voyeurs, the exhibitionists, the S&M lovers, singles, couples, groups, and anyone who could afford a taste in the truly offensive. Also, because of the young appearance of freshly emerged Buds (combined with the fact they were not human, therefore *technically* not children), the business was a resounding hit with those whose predilections tended toward the more youthful end of the age range or who enjoyed perverted 'family' scenes.

With her mind ever on the market forces of supply and demand, 'Chelle had slapped a premium price tag on any Buds with younger-looking offshoots – the price decreasing exponentially as they matured. She had some johns who were happy to pay $50,000 for two immature Buds of the same size before they underwent Separation – more if they were identical. That, however, was as rare to find as a genuine two-headed, albino rattler in a freak show jar.

To cater for the true perverts who craved *something different,* even from fucking conjoined people, 'Chelle and Guidry had brought across a wide spectrum of Buds to meet every taste they'd thought imaginable, and yet the demand was for more and increasingly bizarre combinations of conjoined playthings. Through necessity, Guidry and 'Chelle had become most adept at picking out the most interesting combinations – be it many heads, multiple dicks or/and vaginas, a half dozen breasts... They even learned how to predict a Bud's unopened bulge would turn out, and 'Chelle would attach a price to it before bringing it into her timeline.

One of the more popular attractions – youngsters notwithstanding – was the conjoined man/woman combination. There was just something about the lascivious thrill of a three-way with a permanently attached couple, especially so if said couple sported multiple vaginas and dicks. That had made Kate/Andrew a definite crowd-pleaser; Mhari had separated from them shortly after being brought over, and yet they showed no signs of splitting from each other – such was the randomness of their condition. They had become the most requested conjoined couple because of their depraved nature and exceptional sexual techniques, as well as remaining Guidry's personal playmates.

As for 'Chelle, she had developed quite an addiction for a Bud who had sprouted in such a way that he had four dicks, each one the size of an infant's arm. Three of the cocks were arranged in a neat row across the Bud's crotch, and 'Chelle loved the sensation of two crammed in her cunt and one stuffed up in her ass. The fourth member, which sprouted from her Bud's tongue, 'Chelle loved to stuff her mouth with it and suck on the thing until it spurted hot, sticky come down the back of her throat. Luckily, Guidry was not only okay with that scenario, he *loved* to watch.

The absolute beauty of the Buds was they were constantly budding something new, which kept the brothel's inventory fresh and the clients coming back for more. A conjoined couple, triple, or quadruple would undergo Separation, and each new Bud would sprout new ones practically anywhere and everywhere on their anatomy; it created exciting new collateral, which, of course, meant fewer trips back. The only time that became necessary was once the Buds aged and quit budding to look just like regular, human people.

Perhaps it was Guidry's paranoia over the diminishing time-gap, or maybe just her mercenary tendencies, but 'Chelle was reluctant to waste time taking the spent Buds back. So, she would have them disappear and just tell the others they had returned home, much like one tells a child the family dog that bit the mailman had gone to live on a farm. In reality, 'Chelle had commandeered the long-neglected Guidry family mausoleum at the far reaches of the house's grounds to store the growing pile of dead Bud bodies. Although the deceased Buds fortuitously tended to rot away at a far higher rate than humans, 'Chelle had her people spread the corpses with lye to further expedite decomposition – just to be on the safe side.

She also bet the farm on no one ever visiting the tomb.

As for Guidry – well, he knew better than to ask his girlfriend too many questions.

Suddenly, a shrill, piercing scream shattered the awkward silence in 'Chelle's office. Guidry watched, bemused, as 'Chelle jumped visibly in her chair; he heard its opulent leather creak in protest. The scream rang out again, filled with pain, anguish, and anger; it silenced the hushed voices, ecstatic moans, and orgasmic cries of the brothel.

Guidry and 'Chelle were both on their feet within seconds and they raced from the office.

CHAPTER SEVEN: 0.0007

A commotion was coming from Mhari's room. Although the blood-curdling screams had died down, they had been replaced by irate shouting.

'Chelle burst into the room, Guidry hot on her heels. They were met by a chaotic scene and a most unhappy customer.

"She broke my fucking dick!" The guy on the bed howled. "She fucking *deliberately* broke it!" He was entirely naked, save for a crisscross of leather bondage straps and a black leather gimp mask. He had a hold of his penis in both hands, and 'Chelle saw it was bent in the middle at a ninety-degree angle; blood poured out through his clasped fingers.

She winced on his behalf.

Unfortunately, the gimp in question was one Forrest Bryant, the Police Chief whose blind eye to her operation meant she remained unmolested by the law and therefore in business.

No matter what the circumstances, this did not look good.

Mhari sat huddled and crying in one corner of her room, her twin faces darkened with the beginnings of dark blue bruises on her olive skin. There was a thick snake of blood crawling out from her broken nose.

Mhari had budded a twin head shortly after Separation from Kate/Andrew. Her second head had yet to develop its mouth, but had the most sensual, dark brown eyes imaginable. It also appeared the second head had brought with it some brains because Mhari's previously average intelligence quotient had escalated off the charts upon its arrival. This had made Mhari all the more desirable to 'Chelle's clientele, as it gave her a seemingly endless stream of dark, depraved fantasies she could act out with her paying customers, even though she did resemble the Beeblebrox character from Hitchhiker's.

Like her parents – if that was indeed the correct nomenclature – Mhari had proved a massive hit with 'Chelle's clients, even before her identical head had emerged. Shortly following Separation, she had developed a second pair of legs, between which dangled a formidable penis peppered with lumpy, dripping warts – it resembled a crude sex toy. She'd also sprouted a third breast, along with the torso of an incredibly attractive guy – pretty much a masculine emulation of her beauty – who jutted out from her flank as a fleshy outcrop. The guy had yet to develop his arms, but what he lacked there, he more than made up for with his eager mouth.

It was perhaps the matching, twin vaginas growing on the insides of Mhari's thighs that were her most coveted asset; 'Chelle's clients craved their succulent, wet flesh like it was the finest sweetmeat from the rarest of species. Mhari would slide a dick between her thighs and massage it with the deliciously enveloping flesh of twin pairs of engorged labia – and the suction that the vaginas themselves produced was said to be the most mind-blowing, unbearably pleasurable sensation imaginable. So much so, that only the richest of the brothel's patrons were able to afford the exorbitant fees Mhari commanded.

Richest, or most useful to 'Chelle's operation, which is how one Forrest Bryant could afford Mhari's exquisite talents on a humble Police Chief's salary.

"You'll fucking pay for this, you fucking cunt!" Chief Bryant raged at Mhari as Guidry helped stretcher him out of the room. "I'll fucking kill you and have this *cunting* place shut down – and all you fucking freaks out on the street!" he screamed through his agony.

Guidry tried his best to console the man, and urged his paramedics to get some morphine into the man, *tout* fucking *suite*. The brothel had a team on permanent standby, as many of their clients were elderly and had fragile constitutions – an inordinate number of them required carrying out.

When Bryant was finally out of the room and his rantings were dampened by distance, 'Chelle coaxed Mhari out from her corner and ushered her to the bed. Mhari was clearly shaken – her tear-streaked face a testimony to the ordeal Bryant had subjected her to.

"What happened, Mhari?" 'Chelle's voice was soft, low, and gave the perfect illusion of caring. She plucked a tissue from a box on the nightstand by the bed; the tissue, like its box, was gaily decorated with bright sunflowers and butterflies. 'Chelle wiped away the trickle of blood from Mhari's nose; the girl winced as it brushed her bruised face. "You can tell me. I'm not mad at you, I promise!"

Mhari blinked at her boss through watery eyes, sniffled a fat glob of snot to the back of her throat, and began to talk. As she did so, her twin head simply stared at 'Chelle and her outcrop guy remained silent, although his bruises and the bloodied bite marks on his lumpy dick told their own story.

It transpired that Police Chief Bryant loved to play rough with the Buds. No big secret there: *everyone* knew what a sadist the man was –some Buds refused to entertain him at all – none more so, it seemed, than Mhari. There was just something about her that brought out the violent brute in the man.

Their session had begun with some light spanking. Bryant had spread himself across all four of Mhari's knees, his wobbly white ass in the air, her cock digging into his fat belly. As the spanking got harder – under Bryant's instruction – and his backside redder, he'd become increasingly aroused and, with that, more aggressive.

Once he'd tired of his spanking, Bryant had struggled to his feet to stand over Mhari, his eyes glowering at her through the leather gimp mask he'd brought along for the occasion. "You're a disgusting freak-whore," he'd said.

When Mhari hadn't responded to the insult, he'd slapped her tits as hard as he could with the palm of his meaty hand.

Mhari had heard the insults – and worse – before. Many of her clients (the Police Chief included) would become verbally abusive during their fucking. Some of it was part of their foreplay, some began once the self-loathing kicked in. But this time, there was a tone to Bryant's voice Mhari hadn't much cared for. She'd remained mute and cast a nervous glance at the discrete, red panic button by the bed.

Bryant, angered by Mhari's passive stance, had then balled his fist and launched it at her middle breast.

Mhari had yelped in pain and surprise; she'd felt a *popping* sensation, as if her breast had imploded inside, which made her feel sick to the pit of her stomach. She'd then attempted to stand, but Bryant had knocked her back to the bed with a sharp punch to her nose, and bright twinkling lights had swum through Mhari's vision. She'd grasped his dick and began to stroke it and that had placated Bryant a little – he always liked to see his impressive cock in her delicate hand.

When Bryant knelt down and took Mhari's dick in his mouth, and he was happily slurping it down to the back of his throat, she'd thought the worst was over.

Far from it.

In a fit of rage that apparently came from nowhere, Bryant had bitten down hard on Mhari's dick. She'd kicked out at Bryant and got to her feet, dumping the cop unceremoniously onto the floor.

"You fucking mutant," Bryant had growled as he struggled to his feet, "Just who the fuck do you think you're pushing around?"

And, before Mhari could make a move toward her panic button, Bryant had grabbed her by a fistful of hair and sucker punched her ribs so hard she feared they would snap.

Mhari had never felt so terrified, so vulnerable as she had at that moment. She tried to cry out, but Bryant had silenced her with an expert palm punch to the throat and slammed her face-first into the wall. Still with the grip on Mhari's hair, Bryant had then reached down and forced most of his fist into one of her vaginas and fucked her hard with his hand. When he tired of that, he pinched and tweaked each of her three nipples so hard as to make her squeal, digging his fingernails into the sensitive tissue there to draw tiny droplets of blood.

Finally growing tired of that amusement, Bryant had flung Mhari back onto the bed.

"You're gonna fuck me good 'n hard now, you freaky whore," he'd growled, "and it had better be the best goddamned fuck of my life." He'd laid himself down on the bed beside Mhari and ushered her to climb on top of him.

Mhari had done as instructed, and lowered her third (and normally situated) vagina down onto Bryant's jutting dick and gripped him firmly between her thighs. Her subsidiary vaginas had sucked at his hips like hungry, wet mouths, making his skin sticky with their excretions. She'd never seen Bryant has hard as he was at that moment; beating the crap out of her had certainly floated his sick little boat. And, as she slid her less than lubricated pussy (the rough play had most certainly *not* floated any of Mhari's boats) up and down Bryant's length, he'd batted at her three dangling tits like a recumbent baby playing with its crib mobile.

Bryant had strained himself up to take one of Mhari's sore, bleeding nipples into his mouth and chomped down on it so damned hard it took Mhari's breath away and her vision grayed around the edges.

Angered beyond reason, and in unbearable agony, Mhari had maneuvered her pussy so Bryant's cock was half in, half out, his bulbous meatus buried inside her body. She had then positioned her vagina just so, and with an adroit inward arch of her pelvis, she bore down hard on Bryant's cock.

The Bud hookers in the rooms adjacent to Mhari's – and across the hallway – would all later testify they'd actually heard the snapping noise when Bryant's dick broke; it had the sound of a muffled whip crack, and was accompanied by the most agonized scream any of them had ever heard.

Naturally, Mhari knew enough about the human anatomy to know that, although the penis does not contain any bones, the blood-engorged tissues that create an erection can be just as susceptible to fracturing.

When recounting her story, Mhari omitted the final detail of how she had deliberately broken Bryant's dick. She told 'Chelle it had been a genuine accident, and that such things did happen occasionally, especially with the older men who tended to lose their hard-ons *before* they came.

"He seemed to enjoy the pain." Mhari was crying openly now; her shoulders heaved with each sob. "I thought I was making him happy."

"It's okay, Mhari." 'Chelle stroked the Bud's arm and did her best to reassure, although she knew in her gut it wasn't going to end well.

She really did have no idea.

CHAPTER EIGHT: 0.0005

1.

'Chelle was finding it hard not to giggle.

There was something absurd about the predicament unfolding in her office that brought out the childish schoolgirl in her.

"I really am going to have to insist on some form of compensation," Bryant was talking *at* her, yet all she could focus on was the bulky bulge in the front of his loosely fitting trousers – his splinted, bandaged dick straining to get out. "You can have no idea just how hard this was to explain to Mrs. Bryant," the Police Chief moaned, completely missing his own double entendre.

'Chelle didn't, and stifled another snigger. "I'm sure we can come to some arrangement, Mr. Bryant." She retained just enough composure.

She had to think fast, had to come up with something to appease the arrogant prick before he made good on his promise to bring the full weight of the law down upon her business – but what? The asshole already got everything he wanted for free!

"I want the girl," Bryant answered 'Chelle's silent query.

"Pardon me?"

Guidry chipped in. He'd been sitting quietly, listening to Bryant's disgusting diatribe toward Mhari; he felt uncomfortable the poor Bud had been forced to listen to the man's bullshit too.

"I *said*," Bryant snarled, "I want the fucking girl, or I'm closing down this fucking freak show." He stared intently at Mhari, who offered a thin smile.

"I really don't think –" Guidry countered.

"– I'll go with him," Mhari broke her silence.

"You can't," Guidry said.

"If it's what Mhari wants." 'Chelle looked pleased with the potential resolution to her problem; it was turning out easier than she'd anticipated.

"Then, I think it's for the best."

"You can't be serious," Guidry sputtered. "You know we can't let any Buds outside of the house. How the hell are we supposed to keep all of this quiet?"

"You can rely on my discretion." Bryant looked at each of them with a smile that more resembled a repulsive grimace. "As always."

"And that will be an end to this… *err*, unfortunate incident?" 'Chelle asked.

"Of course, Ma'am."

"Then it's settled," 'Chelle concluded. "Mr. Bryant will take good care of you." She smiled at Mhari.

The Bud's twin head stared wide-eyed at Guidry; the fresh indent where her mouth was soon to be moved in and out with each labored breath. Mhari's conjoined guy peered over her shoulder and shook his head with a sad look in his eyes.

And that was that – problem solved.

Mhari put on her very bravest of faces and went to collect her meager belongings, leaving Guidry to contemplate just what a cold-hearted bitch his girlfriend had become.

2.

There had been tearful, yet brief goodbyes with Kate/Andrew and a few of the other Buds Mhari had made friends with. Then Bryant had ushered Mhari to his car and hurried her away from the brothel with all the urgency of a spoiled kid wanting to get a new toy home.

Mhari had remained passive; she felt guilty she had caused so much trouble for 'Chelle and was wary of reigniting Bryant's wrath. She sat quietly in the cop's German-built SUV and nodded and smiled as he blathered on about nonsense and bullshit – this and that. She said nothing when he turned off of the main road and drove her into the thick forest that sprawled along the edge of town.

"Always wanted to do it in the forest," Bryant said as he eased the car to a halt at the end of a seldom-used logging track. "It's a fantasy of mine." He grinned that dreadful grin of his as he guided Mhari from the car and led her deep into the forest.

Mhari shivered against the early evening chill that caressed her naked skin. She looked nervously around at the closely set, lofty trees with their olive-green leaves and reaching, skeletal branches that seemed to be pointing at her. Above, the dying sun cast strained, orange shafts through the canopy, most of which failed to reach the damp leaf litter on the ground around Mhari's four bare feet.

"You play along and we'll have ourselves a nice time, young lady," Bryant said with a tone to his voice that chilled Mhari's flesh more than any cold breeze ever could.

Before long, they stopped in a small clearing. An old tree had died and toppled over, leaving a gap in the canopy. The tree's corpse and exposed roots lay rotting in the damp air, surrounded by saplings that reached upwards to fill the void. Mhari saw someone had been busy in the soft, exposed dirt by the tree's roots: a freshly dug hole yawned wide in the black soil like the forest had grown a mouth. Next to the hole – blade half-buried into the soil – stood a shovel.

Bryant took careful aim and swung a log at Mhari's unsuspecting, main head. It connected with a satisfying *thwack,* and splinters of mossy bark flew off in all directions like a green halo.

Mhari's eyes rolled upward and back into her head, and she slumped silently to the forest floor.

"Bitch," Bryant muttered as he stepped over his victim.

He aimed a kick at Mhari's twin head that stared up at him with shocked, angry eyes. His heavy boot connected with its temple; the fleshy dent over its mouth heaved in and out. Mhari's offshoot guy wriggled and writhed, as if trying to tear himself free and be away from Bryant's murderous intent, his mute mouth stretched wide in a silent scream.

Bryant plucked the shovel from the dirt as Arthur with his sword, and strode back to Mhari to deliver a flurry of cruel kicks at her three vaginas.

Mhari's eyes shot open and she yelped with pain and surprise. She scrabbled against the soft cushion of decaying leaves and myriad crawling things to escape her attacker.

"This'll teach you to break my fucking dick." Bryant swung the shovel. It smacked Mhari flat side on her jiggling breasts. Again, she screamed out loud, which fueled Bryant's satisfaction even further.

"You like that, don't you?" he sneered. "You like it when I hurt your titties?" He smacked her again, and this time the edge of the shovel sank into the flesh of her right-most breast.

Mhari struggled to get to her feet, to give herself a chance to run.

Bryant guffawed with glee as he knocked Mhari's legs from beneath her with his shovel, slicing a chunk of thigh muscle from one of her three legs as he did so.

Mhari squealed and collapsed to the forest floor.

"There's no use screaming, freak," Bryant said. "There's no one for miles. You may as well man-up and take what's coming to you with good grace." He smacked the shovel against her head, and Mhari's grip on consciousness faltered once more.

Like a thing possessed, Police Chief Bryant danced around Mhari. He amused himself by kicking at her vulnerable, naked body and slamming the shovel down on her flesh to make those delightful smacking sounds. Mhari was out cold again, but her twin head rocked side to side, accusing eyes glaring at him, and mouthing silent screams and threats that held an impotent menace.

Bryant saw the dick swinging between Mhari's legs was stiffening, aroused by the violence he was giving out, and it reminded him of all the times he'd had the throbbing, salty member in his mouth. Oh, how he'd suckled on it like some infant animal at its mother's teat, eagerly gulping down the hot jizz it spasmed into his throat. Filled with self-loathing and envy that the freak's magnificent prick looked far better than his own wrecked cock – Bryant pulled out a small pocket knife and began to slice at Mhari's penis. The knife was quite blunt, so Bryant had to stretch the dick taut with one hand and saw at its base with the dulled blade. As he gripped Mhari's semi-erect cock, the smattering of rough warts adorning it popped and squirted their foul fluid through his fingers.

Growing impatient with his labors, Bryant gripped the dick with both hands, placed his foot on Mhari's crotch and pushed his weight against her. The half-severed dick ripped away from the Bud's body with a wet ripping noise, and Bryant fell back, ass-first onto the ground with the wind knocked from his lungs.

A crimson fountain of blood gushed from the tattered stump of Mhari's penis; her eyes shot wide open and her mouth made an agonized 'O' shape. In unison, her half guy screamed his silent scream and clawed at the ground to rip himself away from the pain. Mhari's twin head opened *her* mouth for the first time. The flimsy skin covering it ripped apart and shreds of bloodied tissue flapped as she let out an ear-splitting ululation that filled the forest with pain.

Bryant let loose with a violent swipe of the shovel and silenced her in an instant.

Mhari's half guy stared at Bryant, eyes filled with rage and hatred, mouth forming obscenities in a language Bryant could never begin to understand. The memories of that wet, welcoming mouth and its oh-so playful tongue served to further enrage Bryant. Snarling like a rabid animal, the Police Chief rained blow upon blow onto the guy's head. Blood, splinters of skull, and chunks of gray-pink brain matter sprayed up and spackled Bryant's face, which gave him a ghoulish appearance as he grunted and wheezed with the exertion of smashing the guy's head to a bloodied pulp.

When it was over, and Bryant's rage had subsided somewhat, Mhari's guy's head was little more than a caved-in mess; one eye had popped out and lay stomped flat in the leaf litter, the other rested in the mouth cavity, lolling on the limp tongue and staring out at the Police Chief. The half-body lay limp and lifeless, jutting out of Mhari's unconscious body like some aborted Frankenstein experiment.

Bryant threw down the shovel and knelt between the pair of Mhari's legs that weren't gushing blood. He pried them apart and plunged his head between her three cunts, twisting his face this way and that to delve his exuberant tongue into each hole in turn to lap up the sweet juices that dribbled from each in a heady liquor of ripe, stinking sex.

When he'd sated his gustatory sense, Bryant kicked off his pants and unbandaged his dick. The doctors had advised that he abstain from any and all sexual activity for at least two months, and looking down at the bruised, purple mess, with the awkward kink in the middle of its shaft, Bryant understood why. He'd seen a post online about some idiot in Europe who'd injected hot Vaseline into his dick to make it bigger, and had wound up needing emergency surgery to save it. The broken thing in his hand reminded him very much of that sorry looking organ.

But, broken penis or no, Bryant simply wasn't going to pass up the opportunity. So, he lowered himself down onto Mhari's bloodied, shattered, lifeless body and, grinding his teeth against the searing pain, he forced his dick into one of her oozing vaginas. Bryant then pumped away into Mhari's cooling corpse; each thrust rocked her limp body and sent jarring agonies through his snapped cock as the broken pieces inside ground against each other. The pain raced from his genitals, up into his guts, and on through his body – until even his goddamned teeth ached.

"Freak," Bryant grunted with each thrust into Mhari, as if he was driving out his self-hatred and disgust with his penis.

"Freak!"

"Freak!"

"Freak!"

And when he'd finished inside Mhari's cunt with a violent ejaculation of stale, clumpy semen and coagulated blood, Bryant rolled her into the shallow grave he'd dug earlier and covered her with dank, earthy soil.

3.

"You have to go back and replace Mhari," 'Chelle told Guidry.

She wriggled her scrumptiously round bottom to better ease the Bud's monstrous dick into her asshole. She gasped as it slipped inside.

"And you know what I think about that," Guidry growled. "We can wait until one of the others separates – it's not like we're short on Buds, 'Chelle." He looked his girlfriend up and down with derision; he'd seen her fucking the Buds before – in the early days of their discovery, they'd shared the creatures on more than one occasion – but what bothered him was he actually didn't give much of a shit that the three-dicked Bud was sliding one of its lengths deep into 'his woman's rectum.

Besides, Guidry had his own dalliances with the Buds; it was a perk of the job. Also, it wasn't as if he and 'Chelle fucked each other anymore. After experiencing the infinite variety and sheer mind-blowing grotesquerie of sex with the Buds, regular human sex just didn't seem to cut it for either of them anymore. On top of that, Guidry didn't want to get his dick out in front of 'Chelle because the tiny warts had spread the length and breadth of it; it looked like an odd, pink, freckled alligator. That, and it hurt and had a seeping rusty-green discharge that stank like something had taken a shit under his foreskin.

"But that could take weeks, months even. And Mhari *was* one of the favorites." 'Chelle's breath came in short spasms as she raised herself up to release the Bud's dick from her ass, the pink tube of her anus splayed wide open. She lowered herself – cunt first – onto the dick, and then bent over to grab both of the Bud's other cocks and cram them into her mouth.

"But the readouts –"

"*Fuck* the readouts!" 'Chelle pulled the cocks out of her mouth. They remained attached to her by thick strings of throat slime. "You either do as I say and get us another – another *Mhari*." 'Chelle rubbed the giant dicks on her tits; her nipples stood, glistening to attention coated in her saliva. "Or I'll fucking do it myself."

Guidry shrugged and scowled at the girl he once would have died for, and wondered at what point in time she had become even more of a mercenary, heartless bitch than she had been before.

'Chelle dismissed Guidry with a cursory wave of the hand and stuffed the cocks back into her mouth and thrust a busy finger up deep into her pouting pussy.

Guidry left the office with a backward glance at the naked, impaled body of the woman he'd once loved more than life itself. He heard her moaning loudly, her cheeks bulging like a greedy hamster's, and Guidry could see the outline of the Bud's oversized dick as it pressed out against the *inside* of her belly. It saddened him to think this was what he and 'Chelle had become.

CHAPTER NINE: 0.0004

1.

In the basement, Guidry stared at the low number on his device's LCD display. It was a lower digit than the last time he'd made a note. *It had to mean something,* he thought, but still couldn't get his head around what.

He could hear the music coming from the sex club above him, *thump – thump – thumping* through the thick wooden door and on down the stairs. The sound comforted Guidry, made him glad to be away from his own timeline, from 'Chelle and the monster she'd become.

Guidry made his way up the stairs, undressing as he went to leave a trail of discarded clothes, Hansel and Gretel-style.

Another plus was he didn't have to be self-conscious about the knobbly appearance of his penis The Buds seemed to quite like it, especially when he buried it deep into their myriad wet, willing holes.

The club was quiet, with only a handful of Buds in attendance. They seemed uncharacteristically sedate for once; standing around in small groups with drinks in their hands, chatting quietly. Guidry thought they had more the air of casual acquaintances standing at a bus stop, waiting.

Guidry made his way through the club toward the exit door He threw a nod and a smile at Carol/Mary/Shannon – a strange Bud he'd fucked the last time he'd visited. They were an odd configuration: all three joined at their breasts and crowns of their heads, which made getting around particularly difficult. Guidry noted they did appear close to undergoing Separation, though, and Mary had sprouted a full, ripe vagina from her cheek.

The streets beyond the club were equally quiet and had a brooding anticipation about them. Except for the occasional bored looking Buds wandering in and out from various stores and brothels – Guidry had the place pretty much to himself.

Behind him, the sex club's facade appeared to shimmer and ripple more than he'd noticed before, and Guidry was certain he could make out the faint outlines of his house in more detail, even down to the silhouetted figures that moved around within. And the trees – the trees dotted around his spacious gardens in his timeline – he saw them as shadows in the streets; some even gave the illusion of protruding from storefronts. Guidry felt as if he could almost reach out and touch them, but something at the back of his mind advised him against it.

Absently, Guidry wandered into a strip joint. He was attracted at a subconscious level by the warm, smoky air and the rank whiff of perspiring flesh. There too, he was immediately aware he was one of only a handful of patrons.

Up on stage was the broad shape of Audrey/Leah – a delightful twin girl Bud with whom he'd enjoyed a dalliance or two during orgies at the club. They comprised two beautifully apportioned bodies joined at the skull; they shared the one eye, three nostrils, and two mouths.

It was the first time Guidry had actually seen them perform, and what a sight it was to behold! They laid on the back they shared, legs spread high in the air as they gyrated their bodies, slender fingers holding open their pussies to display the small, infinitely black holes within their soft folds. Audrey/Leah's dancing was out of time with the background music, slow and lackluster, which reflected perfectly the sparse, unimpressed audience. A fat guy – a rare example of a young, single Bud with nary an offshoot – stood up from his seat in front of the stage and made it rain with what looked to Guidry like a measly eight bucks. Fat Guy paused with an expectant look on his face, hopeful he would be invited onto the stage to participate as others had before him.

Audrey/Leah ignored him and kissed each other full on the mouth, all four hands busy at the twin vaginas they shared, tiny breasts pressed hard against each other.

Eventually, the fat guy sat down and slurped at his beer, much of it dribbling down his front.

The music stopped.

Audrey/Leah climbed down from the stage, taking great care to circumnavigate the fat guy, who looked at them disgruntled as he mumbled incoherently into his drink.

"Hi, Wildus," Audrey greeted Guidry as she would an old friend.

"Hey," Guidry replied, his mind elsewhere.

"It's been a while," Leah said.

"I've been busy," Guidry offered by way of an explanation.

"We thought you'd forgotten us." Audrey giggled.

Guidry studied the beautiful creatures and wondered how they could ever think such a thing. *How could anyone forget the immensely pleasurable fellatio they provided with those twin mouths?*

The twins pawed at one another's pointy breasts as they spoke, tweaking fiercely erect nipples and kneading the pliant flesh. Guidry saw that just how aroused they were from their performance; those vaginas were full-lipped, wet, and ready for fucking.

"Are you looking for sex?" Leah, as direct as Guidry remembered her, asked.

"*Err*, no… I mean, *yes*," Guidry stammered.

"I mean, I'm looking for someone to take back."

"Really?!" Leah/Audrey said in unison. "We thought you'd never ask!"

Guidry was surprised at their ebullience, and even more so at the sick, sinking feeling it gave him in the pit of his stomach. The memory of Mhari's distraught face as she'd left 'Chelle's office earlier that day, coupled with the likelihood she was unlikely to ever return, made Guidry hesitant.

"You don't think we're suitable?" Leah sensed Guidry's reluctance.

"It's not that," Guidry struggled. "It's more –"

"Meet Sandra." Audrey/Leah chimed in unison and turned around. There, budding from Audrey's back, was a teenaged girl, who certainly hadn't been there the last time Guidry had around. The girl's face emerged from just below Audrey's neck, the nubs of her pubescent breasts from the middle of her host's rib cage, the protruding bones of her pelvis from her buttocks, and the bulging mound of her bare pussy neatly in the center. Sandra had the outlines of hands pressed against the inside of Audrey's skin, and her legs bulged out from the back of Audrey's legs. Sandra smiled at Guidry, and he nodded hello; he just couldn't get it out of his head how much she reminded him of Han Solo frozen in carbonite at the end of the second Star Wars movie.

"We heard there's a premium for youngsters," Leah said.

"*Yeah,* and Sandra is a horny little bitch. Ain't that right, San'?" Audrey laughed.

"Yes, Ma'am," Sandra agreed with a child-like reverence. "What do you say, Mr. Guidry?"

Guidry contemplated the naked delights presented to him, watched a lazy trickle of brown-streaked come slide from between Leah's buttocks and on down the back of her thigh – it would seem there had been *some* audience participation that night. Perhaps Audrey/Leah/Sandra would make a suitable substitution for Mhari? Although they didn't have a dick to offer, they possessed that most coveted of all attributes for 'Chelle's brothel – young flesh.

As he contemplated transporting Audrey/Leah/Sandra back to his timeline, Guidry had a reality attack.

What the fuck was going on here?

He was catering for sick perverts who had a taste in the bizarre and young bodies, dealing with the increasingly unpleasant thing 'Chelle had become, the cynical exploitation of what should have been an earth-shattering discovery, all overshadowed by the undeniable fate of poor Mhari.

"I – I'm sorry, I can't." Guidry backed away from Audrey/Leah/Sandra, realizing he *really* couldn't do this, not anymore. "I have to go." Turning tail, Guidry ran from the strip joint and back toward the club, his diseased dick bouncing heavily against his thighs.

2.

Guidry felt cornered, the basement – once his sanctuary – felt like its walls were closing in as 'Chelle's wrath poured down upon him like toxic rain.

"What the fuck do you mean? You *couldn't*?!" she ranted. "I sent you to do one thing, Wildus, one *motherfucking* thing!" She stood toe-to-toe with Guidry, her taller stature most intimidating at such close range.

"I decided it would be a bad idea." Guidry felt proud of himself for standing up to 'Chelle, although doing so naked and with his head still spinning from the trip back was probably not the best timing. Between 'Chelle's shouting, the immense Bud she'd brought down with her to guard the door, and the cold air in the basement, Guidry's skin prickled with gooseflesh and his warty dick had shriveled to near-maggot proportions. Luckily, he had the device to hide that particular disgrace.

"You decided!?" 'Chelle yelled. "You fucking *decided*?" Speckles of saliva flew from her mouth and splashed on Guidry's bare chest. It was warm and moist, and in different circumstances, it would have turned him on.

"Look at the readout, 'Chelle." He twisted the device around so she could see the LCD display while still keeping his cock hidden.

Guidry let 'Chelle stare at the figures on the display, although he knew she had no idea what she was supposed to be looking at. To be truthful, he was none the wiser, but the 0.0001 worried him; any lower and the display would simply show *ERROR*.

"So?" 'Chelle displayed her ignorance. "What does it mean, Wildus?" her voice was taunting, cruel.

"I – I don't know," Guidry was forced to admit.

'Chelle rolled her eyes, put a hand on her hip, and thrust out her pelvis. Guidry thought she looked like a tall, ebony teapot. "We really have to stop using it, 'Chelle." Guidry's voice was quiet and shaky. "Can't you *feel* something's wrong here?"

"What I'm feeling right now, Wildus, is the fucking big Mhari-shaped hole in our profit margins," 'Chelle sneered. "A hole we have to fill – and fill quickly."

Guidry allowed himself a wry smile at 'Chelle's unintended pun and lifted the time travel device above his head, no longer caring 'Chelle would see his diseased prick; he made ready to smash the infernal thing on the concrete floor.

"No!" 'Chelle cried out; a look of absolute panic drained her face.

Guidry felt the device turn inexplicably heavy in his hands, a smooth, hard knee in his back, and he crashed to the floor. He twisted around and landed hard on his ass, and the wind was knocked from his lungs with an audible *oof.*

Looking up, he saw the vast bulk of 'Chelle's henchman towering over him. He was broad, naked, and glistening, his three dicks in their permanent state of semi-erection and at eye level with Guidry. Three-Dicks held the device in his fat, muscular hands. He turned it over a couple of times, as if trying to work out in his dim brain where the batteries went, and then handed it over to 'Chelle.

"I'll look after this, Wildus," 'Chelle growled. "Since you can't be trusted."

Guidry looked up at his girlfriend. He could barely recognize the woman he'd let into his life with such open arms; she had become as ugly on the inside as she was beautiful on the outside, her exquisite face now a mask of pure avarice and contempt. From his position on the chilly floor, Guidry saw far enough up the blue leather mini skirt she wore to see 'Chelle had forgone panties. He could also see the lumps and bumps of the multitude of tiny warts that dotted her pink, protruding pussy lips, and he wondered if hers had tiny faces too.

"Take him away," 'Chelle barked at Three-Dicks. "I don't want to see his stupid face for the rest of the day. You might as well lock him in Mhari's old room, seeing as though it's still fucking empty." She just couldn't resist one more dig.

The giant Bud lifted Guidry up by his underarms so abruptly his shoulders popped and he yelped at the sudden stab of pain. Once on his feet, the Bud frogmarched Guidry toward the basement door, leaving 'Chelle contemplating the device he'd fashioned out of their sex toy.

"For Christ's sakes, don't use it, 'Chelle," Guidry called over his shoulder. He wanted to stop and talk to her – rational person to rational person – but his escort kept him walking; all the while, Guidry felt the Bud's monstrous cocks banging against his buttocks, as if requesting entry.

"Don't tell me what to do, Wildus," 'Chelle snarled. "And what the fuck happened to your dick?"

Guidry looked down at his sorry member, a minnow in comparison to the thick, twelve-inch cocks that swung between the henchman's legs. It was now thoroughly covered in tiny brown warts, and the suppurating stink coming off of it was quite nauseating. And, he noticed, some of the minuscule faces were winking and smiling at him.

But, before Guidry could answer, before he could add the mysterious genital disease to his *fucking good reasons not to go back to Budworld* argument, Three-Dicks had ushered him through the door at the top of the stairs, and out of the basement.

3.

The forest was lightless, cold, and damp when Mhari clawed her way out of the shallow grave Police Chief Bryant had so thoughtfully dug out of the forest floor for her.

There was only just the slightest glimmer of a half-moon shimmering through the breeze-tossed branches above her, and Mhari could hear the rustle and dry-leaf crunch of the night creatures going about their business as she grunted with the exertion of hauling her bodies out of the ground. Her twin head remained unconscious from Bryant's beating, and her offshoot-guy was as dead as they come; his head was smashed beyond all recognition and clogged up with congealed blood, splintered skull bone, and bits of leaf litter. It made his body a limp, dead weight that pulled harshly on the flesh of Mhari's back and made her cry out in pain.

Sitting still awhile to catch her breath and spit out the clogs of dirt that had filled her mouth and pull out the bloated earthworms that had crawled up her vagina, Mhari could smell her dead offshoot was already beginning to decay – the process no doubt hurried along by the clammy conditions below the forest floor. And as she struggled to her feet, Mhari felt the half-corpse flopping against her bare skin to paint it with smears of stale blood and sticky clumps of brain.

Mhari turned her head away from the stink and filled her lungs with the chilled night air. She put on her most determined face and began walking in the direction of the Guidry house. The filtered moonlight lit her face a silvery shade of pale, and she looked just like a ghost.

CHAPTER TEN: 0.0001

1.

It was a busy night, which meant 'Chelle's mind was kept occupied. There seemed to be a predominance of Mhari's regular clients who were all asking for their special Bud – *what was it about Sunday nights?*

Whilst it grieved her to offer discounts and keep VIP clients waiting, 'Chelle found it gratifying her clientele were willing to a man (and a couple of the ladies, too) to put up with the inconvenience of forgoing their favorite delicacy and being forced to pick out an alternative playmate. She supposed it was inevitable though; after all, where the fuck else could they go for what she offered?

Still, 'Chelle plotted.

There was an empty room that needed filling if she was to maintain her bottom line; perhaps she could provide her clients with a specimen even more exotic that the ever-popular Mhari?

Which brought 'Chelle back to Wildus.

He remained locked in Mhari's vacated room, hopefully stewing over the implications of his insubordination. If 'Chelle was forced to use the device herself, Guidry knew just how much more pissed she would be at him; 'Chelle hated visiting Budworld, as she found the place dirty and depressing, while the trip itself gave her a nausea that took days to shift.

But, if Wildus couldn't be trusted to follow simple instructions and was in danger of destroying the machine that had provided them with so much – *instant* – wealth, then 'Chelle would have no choice but to take the trip herself, no matter how much she detested the idea.

"*Don't stop…*" 'Chelle murmured, and the two-headed girl between her legs went back to snaking busy tongues into her sopping cunt. 'Chelle leaned back in her office chair and allowed the waves of pleasure to ripple through her body, closing her eyes to let the warm, undulating sensations carry her away from the bitch of a day she'd been having.

She had no clue it was about to get a hell of a lot worse.

2.

Police Chief Bryant relaxed on the bed and took in the private floorshow the two sets of Buds were laying on for him; each pairing was conjoined at the chest and hip. He'd ordered – no, *demanded* – two of 'Chelle's most beautiful female-male combinations, and was now making them fuck each other for his delectation. Of course, being the sick fuck he was, Bryant had insisted one of the girls wear a monstrously oversized strap-on to fuck the other girl, whilst the guys fucked each other up the ass; the four bodies actually fitted together like some porn film jigsaw puzzle.

There was also the added attraction of the small bud that sprouted from the middle of one of the couple's backs. It was a half-formed girl with long, shiny-black hair, who looked to be no more than ten or twelve.

Bryant had returned directly to the brothel after dispatching Mhari, having made the decision not to go home to face more awkward questions from his hag of a wife. He'd taken advantage of the luxurious showers to clean up, and had disposed of the severed dick he'd kept in his pocket down one of the brothel's toilets. It had bled out and shriveled to nothing, and was no longer of interest to Bryant.

The Buds fucked each other with fake – but *very good* fake – enthusiasm. Bryant toyed with his dick despite (*because of?*) the intense pain that shot from it with each stroke and the worrying way in which it bent at a peculiar angle in the middle. Sure, the doctor had told him to stay off the thing to avoid permanent damage, but what the fuck? He had money, and the docs could fix it up again. Hell, they even transplanted the damn things nowadays – so there was even the possibility of picking himself out a nice new one, maybe even treat himself to a fat, black one, so he could split some of 'Chelle's freaky bastards in two.

Now, there would be an experience second to none. Perhaps it would be even better than smashing their brains in with a shovel?

The Buds were reaching their inevitable crescendo, and Bryant could feel he was close to his own climax, although he was not too sure as to how he would be able to ejaculate – his dick had swollen even more since he'd fucked Mhari's corpse in the forest, and the angle of its bend more acute.

One of the Bud guys was busy licking Bryant's cock with the mouth that stuck out from his left thigh. He lapped at the cops' thrusting dick as it slid in and out of the other guy's ass, his tongue cleaning off the flecks of shit that were dragged out by its shaft. Meanwhile, his conjoined woman rammed the thick latex cock into her opposite number with gusto, oblivious to the woman's pained groans and the fact she could clearly see the delicate vaginal tissues were beginning to tear. Blood streaked the flesh-toned dildo, and the coppery scent of fresh blood wafted out into the air.

Unable to contain himself any longer, Bryant clambered from the bed to join the couples, his crooked dick hard, angry, and inflamed. He lifted up the arm of the strap-on woman and aimed his dick at the juicy vagina that resided in her armpit.

The Bud obliged, of course, and sighed as Bryant sank his broken dick deep inside her armpit pussy. She brought her arm down to clamp him tight, and Bryant let out a wail that was agony and ecstasy all rolled up into one ugly, chilling sound.

Bryant grimaced against the intense pain and tried to focus on the pleasure that the vagina – and the pain – were giving him. He rocked his hips back and forth to fuck the Bud as she fucked the other woman while the guys sodomized each other.

This was absolute, fucking heaven.

He didn't notice the door behind him open.

Mhari shuffled into the room, her legs stiff from the long, arduous walk back from the forest. Her back was crooked from carrying the weight of the flopping corpse of her half-guy, who had soiled himself inside of her when Bryant had caved in his head; his excrement oozed out from Mhari's trio of vaginas, which made a stink that wrinkled the poor gal's nose. Her twin head was conscious now, and she stared with murderous intent at Bryant through the dried blood caked over her face.

Bryant caught a whiff of the rank stench and turned his head. But, by then, Mhari was upon him.

Mhari threw her arms around Bryant, which took him completely by surprise and lifted him away from the Buds with whom he was cavorting. Bryant opened his mouth to scream his protest, but Mhari pressed his face into her chest and filled his gaping maw with her middle breast; she barely even flinched as Bryant bit down hard on her soft flesh –the pain served only to further inflame her fury.

Forcing Bryant to the floor, Mhari wrapped her legs around his, and Bryant could feel her vaginas hot and wet and sucking at his thighs. He felt them draw in his flesh in a perverse love-bite, the blood vessels rupturing, and his blood flowing freely into Mhari's hungry cunts. As he fought to be free, Bryant also felt the bloodied gristle of the stump between the Bud's second pair of legs, where the dick had been before he'd ripped it off. It dug hard into his leg as he struggled against Mhari's suffocating weight and chomped down again on the tit that invaded his mouth; he tasted blood.

Mhari clawed at Bryant's pudgy flesh, her sharp nails drawing long lines of blood and ragged skin behind them. She relished the muffled vibration of his screams against her chest and his struggles against her weight, which became ever more frenetic as she stifled the breath from him. But, as she sucked the blood and life from her victim, Mhari's strength grew – Bryant didn't stand a chance against her.

The Buds in the room approached Mhari and Bryant and circled like beta dogs at a pack's kill. Mhari and her twin head nodded their assent, and the Buds fell upon Bryant with a savage blood lust.

Quickly, the Buds and Mhari tore Bryant apart; they stuffed the bloodied clods of his flesh into their mouths, while their dicks invaded his body and hungry vaginas slurped on his flesh. Weakened, Bryant kicked out his legs and lashed out blindly with feeble arms, but his blows deterred none of the assailants. Even when he bit her nipple clean off and gagged when it lodged in his throat, Mhari didn't relinquish her hold on the perverted cop who'd left her for dead.

3.

Meanwhile, in the absence of anything else to do, Guidry had been napping in Mhari's old room. He awoke at the sound of the commotion in the hallway and sat bolt upright on the king-sized bed; he strained his ears at the noise of shouting and feet running along the hardwood floors. There was no way he could go investigate, as 'Chelle's henchman – the three-dicked fuck-toy – had locked the door from the outside. 'Chelle had fitted all of the bedroom doors with locks back in the brothel's formative days – long before they knew the Buds had no intention of attempting to escape.

At first, Guidry thought he was hearing just another one of 'Chelle's orgy free-for-alls, in which the Buds were allowed out of their rooms and everyone congregated in the newly refurbished ballroom for sex and debauchery. More often than not, the licentiousness overflowed into the hallways and beyond, as clients chased after Buds who pretended to run away from them – it was all part of the game.

But then he heard the screams.

They were most definitely not screams of delight and sexual pleasure, but rather screams of pain and terror. Alarmed, Guidry shuffled from the bed, and suddenly, the door burst open, swinging wildly on its bent hinges. For a moment, Guidry feared the door was going to separate from its frame completely and crash down on him.

"Mhari!" He was shocked at the state of the intruder, and all at once painfully aware of his nakedness. The once beautiful offshoot of Kate/Andrew was now a stinking, bloodied mess; her skin was caked with blood – some old, most of it new – and dirt. Mhari's center breast was a raw,

bleeding wound with an ugly, ragged hole where the nipple had once been, and her vaginas oozed blood streaked with fecal matter. Guidry gasped in horror when he realized she was carrying the corpse of her offspring on her back, his ruined head lolling side to side as she walked into the room.

"Hello, Wildus." Mhari's voice was thick, liquid.

"I thought you'd –"

"– you were mistaken." Mhari took another step toward Guidry. In her wet, bloodied hand, she carried what appeared to be a large dick. It was the purple-yellow of old bruises – and was bent in its middle at a most unnatural angle.

Behind Mhari, Guidry espied the growing chaos in the hallway: crimson-smeared Buds chased panicking, terror-filled people, and thick sprays of blood were redecorating 'Chelle's expensive, imported wallpaper.

"H – he did this to you?" Guidry felt sick to his stomach. "Bryant, I mean"

Mhari nodded.

There was a soulful sadness displayed in her eyes that Guidry had yet to see in a Bud. "You sent me away with him. You *knew* what he was going to do to me."

"No, no no." Guidry shook his head. "It was all 'Chelle's idea –

to keep Bryant quiet about what you did to him."

"Well, he's quiet now, alright." Mhari threw Bryant's severed dick at Guidry. It hit him square on the sternum and left a bloodied mark on his chest. Mhari took another step and grabbed Guidry's arm. She pulled him toward her grimy, bloodied chest with an unyielding hand to the back of his head.

Guidry struggled against Mhari's grip, but she was far too strong for him, preternaturally so. He saw her wobbling, bulbous breasts looming, and felt claustrophobic panic as the flesh pressed hard against his face and blocked off his breathing. He beat his hands against Mhari and kicked at her thighs, could feel the slick warmth of her vaginas grasping at his legs.

"Mhari! *No!*" a voice rang out, and Guidry felt the grip on his skull relax a little; he was able to take in a gulp of fetid air.

"Let him go, Mhari." a second voice instructed; Kate/Andrew had come to Guidry's rescue.

Mhari relinquished her grip, and Guidry plopped down heavy on the floor at her feet – the much-needed gasp of air was knocked from his lungs with a wheezing snort.

"What did they do to you?" Kate's voice was filled with mother's anguish.

"They sent me out to die," Mhari said, her eyes brimming with tears. "I can't let them get away with that."

"He's not the one you want," Andrew told her. "He's weak-willed and pussy-whipped." He pointed at Guidry, who looked offended.

"It's the woman who allowed this to happen," Kate added. "She's the one who deserves your anger."

As Mhari stepped back from Guidry, he saw Kate/Andrew in the doorway. Behind them, in the hallway, a three-woman Bud had hold of a screaming, elderly woman and was busy tearing the floppy tits off her scrawny chest and chowing down like it was her last meal.

And then Mhari was gone. She shambled off along the hallway with all four legs moving apace, barging into and through anyone who got in her way. She almost tripped up over the writhing, gory mess of a disemboweled young woman and a Bud intent upon ripping the pierced inner labia away from her pussy.

"Thank you." Guidry forced a smile at Kate/Andrew as they stepped inside the room and closed the door behind them the best they could. It jammed in the doorframe; a couple of screws fell out of its hinges and bounced on the carpet.

"We couldn't let her kill you." Andrew smiled. "You're far too useful."

"That's good to know," Guidry replied, although he couldn't for the life of him think why.

"But that woman of yours," Kate sighed, "well, she's a different matter altogether."

"We can't let Mhari hurt 'Chelle." Guidry scrabbled to his feet.

"Why not, Wildus?" Andrew appeared most puzzled. "After everything she's done to you, to *us*?"

"Andrew's right," Kate chipped in. "Best let what is going to happen, happen."

Kate/Andrew ushered Guidry back to the bed and had him sit. From outside the room, Guidry heard the screams and shouts and the rending of human flesh as the chaos grew.

4.

'Chelle Tran *harrumphed* with impatience. The commotion in the house was disturbing her pleasure, and she knew she'd never reach orgasm with her mind distracted. Added to that, she couldn't remember signing off on an orgy – Thursdays were orgy nights.

"You're gonna have to stop that," she growled at the Bud, who was dutifully slurping away at her pussy, and had all four hands busy away on her tits. "I *really* can't concentrate with all that noise going on." 'Chelle thrust her crotch into her playmate's mouths to push them away. The Bud sat back heavily on her ass, faces shiny, wet, and streaked with menstrual blood. 'Chelle stood up, slipped her heels back on, and smoothed down her skirt.

"Don't go anywhere," she instructed the Bud. "I'm not finished yet." As if it was news to the poor Bud – she'd been busy licking at 'Chelle's cunt for over an hour to no avail. The Bud looked up with a forced smile on each of her bloodied faces.

'Chelle stormed out of her office. Nothing much irked her more than being left with her itch unscratched, and there was something about period days that made her even hornier.

Beyond the cocoon of 'Chelle's office, it was pandemonium. Her clientele were out of the playrooms and openly fornicating with Bud hookers in the hallway, the dining room, and the lounge. There were also sounds coming from the kitchen that were unmistakably *sex*. The impromptu orgy taking place was very reminiscent of the clubs 'Chelle and Guidry had patronized in Budworld, with all their wanton displays of sexual abandon and exhibitionism.

By her office door, a pair of Buds – one of three guys joined at the chest, one of three girls joined at the head and sharing five eyes – were sandwiching an oriental couple, who had a look on their faces as if they'd died and gone to erotic heaven. The guy, who 'Chelle recognized as the CEO of some big, global car company, had his dick buried to the hilt in his wife's ass while she traded wet tongue kisses with the girls. The guys were each fucking one of the girls, thrusting in unison and making a rough rhythm that eased CEO guy in and out of his woman; each thrust made her squeal with delight.

To her left, 'Chelle saw one of her brothel's favorites receiving cunnilingus from two men on the billiard table. The Bud's succulent vaginas – one between her legs, one between the legs that sprouted from between her breasts – engulfed the men's faces as they slurped down the thick, stringy mucus that seeped out of the pink, swollen flesh. And all the while, a young man's head beneath her armpit looked on with a serene smile.

Everywhere 'Chelle looked it was the same: sweating, fucking, naked bodies, Buds on Buds, Buds with men and/or women, or both, married couples swapping partners with Buds and other married couples, cocks buried deep in puckered asses, insertions in dripping cunts of dicks, fists and feet, mouths dribbling semen and stuffed full of cock or suffocating against vaginas; the entire place positively *reeked* with the stink of raw flesh and bodily fluids. And, amongst the debauchery, the cries of pleasure were rapidly turning to those of pain, blood was beginning to flow, flesh being torn, and then 'Chelle saw –

"Oh, shit." she muttered beneath her breath as Mhari strode purposefully toward her through the cavorting bodies.

The Bud's twin heads were turned directly at 'Chelle, all four eyes glowering with determination.

'Chelle took a moment or two to comprehend the fact it *was* the Mhari she'd sent away with the violent sociopath Police Chief, and she understood Mhari's return didn't bode well for her at all. Terrified, 'Chelle ducked back into her office as Mhari broke into a run and within seconds was was pounding on the office door quicker than her ungainly stature would have suggested.

"Help me," 'Chelle said to the Bud, who not five minutes ago had been tongues-deep in her vagina. "I'll give anything you want. *Please!*" There was genuine panic in 'Chelle's voice, a tremble that broke her words.

The door burst in as Mhari's weight snapped the lock; it swung crazily on its hinges. "Where is she?" She growled at the Bud. "I know she's in here."

"We don't know," the Bud's heads said in unison, naked breasts heaving defiance. But her eyes – all four – gave the game away. They twitched ever so slightly toward the desk beneath which 'Chelle was cowering.

Mhari was in the mood for revenge, not bullshit. She aimed two of her four knees at the Bud's genitals and brought them up with such force her target's bare feet lifted off the ground. The Bud collapsed to the floor with a winded grunt and threw up thick, yellow vomit as both heads bounced hard on the floor. As Mhari's attention was momentarily distracted, 'Chelle seized her chance: she grabbed Guidry's time travel device and cell phone from her desk and ran for the door.

Mhari reacted in an instant, but the collapsed Bud at her feet put distance between her and the retreating 'Chelle. All Mhari managed to do was grab wildly at 'Chelle's hair as the woman fled the office.

'Chelle yelled out in pain as a clump of her hair was ripped out by its roots. For a split second, she feared she'd been caught, and was in fact almost relieved when she felt her scalp give way. Blood poured down the back of her neck as she dodged this way and that, jumping and weaving between the romping, naked, bleeding bodies, desperate to be away from Mhari, who lumbered after her with hate in her eyes.

In the kitchen – the basement door in sight – 'Chelle jumped over a Bud, who was both female and male, conjoined at the waist with a shared navel. It had no legs and maneuvered solely by use of four muscular arms; its female half had a full, gaping vulva growing from the side of her head, just above the ear. A skinny, middle-aged guy who had been fucking the vagina pulled out as 'Chelle ran toward him, scared he'd be trampled mid-coitus. As he did so, the Bud gushed a veritable tsunami of green-gray juice from the pussy, which soaked her, her partner, and their client.

'Chelle's foot landed square in the slippery puddle of mucus and it slid from under her. She fell with little grace and landed legs in the air – fresh-shaven pussy for all to see – on top of the Bud. Guidry's device flew from her hands and skittered away across the tiled floor.

She'd felt bones crunch beneath her weight, and the Bud that had broken 'Chelle's fall on was no longer moving. The guy who had been screwing the pouting vagina looked on, horrified, his dick wilting, but 'Chelle had no time for sympathy; Mhari was so close she could smell the sickly-sweet, decaying stink emanating from her.

'Chelle scrabbled her feet against the slippery floor, expensive shoes flying off in opposite directions. Barefooted, she managed to gain purchase on the tiles and drag herself back upright. Looking down, she saw the twisted, squashed body of the double-torso Bud she had fallen upon; it looked incredibly dead, *deflated*.

Mhari grabbed 'Chelle's arm and pulled on it with such force the *crack* her shoulder joint made resounded around the kitchen and distracted the resident fornicators from their business.

'Chelle yelped and lashed out with her free hand. Her fist connected with Mhari's nose, and she felt with satisfaction the already broken cartilage *smush* and a warm gush of blood splash her knuckles. Mhari's middle arm grasped for 'Chelle, its fingers curled into vicious claws. It closed in on her breast and grasped it so tight 'Chelle feared it would burst.

"Bitch!" 'Chelle clawed at Mhari's eyes as searing pain from her assaulted tit threatened to drive her into unconsciousness.

Mhari twisted her heads away from 'Chelle's grasping fingers, her boss's French manicured nails just fractions of an inch away from her eyes. She retained a tight grip on her quarry, relishing 'Chelle's futile squirming and the feel of her own fingers buried in the soft breast tissue.

She was determined to enjoy this.

An obese man burst through the kitchen door, his pale rolls of fat wobbling as he waddled with an ungainly gait. Behind him walked a slender, petite Bud, a young girl with an even younger girl growing out from between her breasts. Both girls were crying and had trails of blood along the insides of their thighs – and the fat man had blood on his tiny acorn prick.

"Coming through!" Obese Man blustered as he led the girls through the kitchen. His lard ass barged straight into Mhari and he almost knocked her over.

Mhari's grip loosened on both 'Chelle's arm and, to much relief, her tit, and she wriggled free. Mhari grasped at 'Chelle's chest again, but this time caught only her dress. As 'Chelle pulled back, it gave way with a loud tearing noise; several people in the kitchen looked over admiringly, as if witnessing some violent, sexy role play.

'Chelle left Mhari clutching the top of her dress – *twelve-hundred dollars, pure silk import!* – with a bemused look on one face and an angry expression aimed at the fat man on the other. Seizing her chance, 'Chelle dashed, topless, across the kitchen.

Retrieving the device from between the copulating bodies, she headed toward the basement door.

CHAPTER ELEVEN: *ERROR*

1.

'Chelle slammed the basement door shut behind her; she knew the flimsy lock wouldn't hold Mhari for long and her only chance of escape was Guidry's device. 'Chelle planned to skip over to Budworld and wait for Mhari to either give up the chase or die – surely the wretched creature couldn't carry a rotting corpse around with her forever?

It had crossed 'Chelle's mind to use the device in her office, but then she'd remembered Guidry always insisted on taking the trips from the same spot in the basement. He'd tried his best to explain it to her in layman's terms, but all she'd gathered from his lengthy monologue – *with diagrams* – was the basement was a constant between the two timelines and the danger of using a different location to travel between the two was of winding up entombed inside a wall, or with your head buried in a tree or some such.

'Chelle placed the device on the ground in its usual spot on the floor and fished Guidry's cell phone from her pocket. She then wriggled what remained of her dress down over her hips and stood there naked with the cool air plucking gooseflesh the length and breadth of her body.

The door at the top of the steps crashed open and, as predicted, the tiny brass lock was torn easily from the frame. It fell down the stairs in pieces, each part tinkling musically as it bounced.

Mhari bustled down the stairs, her twin faces seething masks of hate.

"Don't you fucking dare!" she bellowed at 'Chelle.

Ignoring the furious Bud, 'Chelle poked a panicked finger at Guidry's cell phone, desperately searching for the app that worked his infernal machine. She'd observed over his shoulder on many of their trips to Budworld, and was confident she could get the device to work; if only she could find where he kept the app on his goddamned phone.

Mhari descended the basement stairs with more grace than four legs and a rotting corpse on her back should have allowed; her putrescent stink very quickly filled the confined space. She eyed 'Chelle, taking in the woman's tall, slim body and incredibly sexy, denuded pudendum. Mhari had always loved that part of 'Chelle, had never been able to get enough of its taste and how it felt closed in around her fingers.

But now, all Mhari could see was the woman who had discarded her like an unwanted pet to save her disgusting business and her own flawless skin. She rushed across the basement with ever intent of exacting her revenge once and for all, determined to make 'Chelle suffer for everything she'd done to her and her people.

'Chelle coughed at the stench clawing at her throat and making her eyes water. Blinking away the tears, she prodded at the cell phone with increased ferocity; Guidry's app *had* to be there somewhere.

"Gotcha!" she exclaimed.

Guidry had buried the app's thumbnail in a folder he'd named 'HGW' – no doubt a cack-handed homage to Wells' *Time Machine.*

"Don't!" Mhari screamed from less than three strides away.

"Fuck you, bitch!" 'Chelle laughed as she pressed the *Go* button with her thumb.

2.

There was the familiar *pushing*, which felt like her guts were trying to escape, along with the hot sensation between her legs as her vagina juiced up; its fluids trickled down her legs. The world swam nebulous and milky around her, and the accompanying mini-lightning flashes had her squeezing her eyes tight shut as high-pitched shrieks assaulted her ears.

And then there came the *jolt.*

Like a sudden stop in an automobile, the jarring halt signaled the end of the jaunt. 'Chelle breathed a sigh of relief.

Opened her eyes.

"Fuck!"

"Fuck, indeed," Mhari echoed.

'Chelle's mind raced; had Mhari somehow hitched a ride, despite having been not close enough to the device? Or – worst scenario of all – had the device failed? 'Chelle looked down at the digits on the LED display on the thing that lay by her bare feet.

ERROR

Mhari grabbed 'Chelle with all three arms and coiled her outermost legs around her thighs to trap her in a grotesque bear hug.

"Let me go!" 'Chelle snarled her protest and struggled; the stink seeping off of the Bud was so strong her vision swam in and out, as if she were viewing her attacker through a heat haze.

Mhari responded by forcing one hand down between their bodies. In an instant, her crawling fingers searched out 'Chelle's moist sex; she beamed with delight as they found their target and 'Chelle let out an involuntary *ohh*.

'Chelle struggled against Mhari the best she could, but found herself hopelessly outweighed. As she fought, she dropped Guidry's phone on the hard floor, where it clattered into a dozen pieces. Wriggling her body against the Bud's tight grip, she hoped that her sweat, mixed with Mhari's coating of slime, blood, and God-only-knows-what, would give her the lubricity to slither free like a wily old eel. But, with each probe of Mhari's fingers at her sex, 'Chelle's resolve lessened: the Bud knew her victim's body all too well and was actually finger-fucking 'Chelle into submission.

By the time her fourth finger and thumb were inserted deep inside 'Chelle's vagina, Mhari felt 'Chelle's body growing limp, her struggles less urgent. One last push upward – her hand well lubricated by 'Chelle's overactive Bartholin's glands – followed by a grab and pull –

– 'Chelle roared out her agony as Mhari pulled her inside out; the slippery wetness of her vagina and its adjoining organs slopped out against her thighs to slide hot and wet onto her feet. A cascade of blood and thick globs of innards followed as 'Chelle's body emptied out through her vagina, and the last things she saw as her life drained away like puke down a plug hole were Mhari's twin heads smiling at her.

3.

Guidry's time travel device hadn't failed at all. In fact, Guidry knew at what point exactly it *had* worked, as did everyone else on the planet.

Kate/Andrew had been keeping him occupied the best way they knew how after saving him from Mhari's manic clutches. With Andrew's encouragement, Kate had treated Guidry's misshapen, lumpy penis to the special thing she did with her ass.

The rectal prolapse was something of a party piece for Kate: she could protrude the resplendent red flesh of her rectum at will, and it would bulge out like a giant, exotic sea anemone. Not only that, but she could make it envelop a dick and massage it into paroxysms of euphoria with little more than rhythmic tensing of her sphincter muscles.

Guidry had been close to climax when *it* had happened. He'd experienced the room – the *world* – shift, and everything around him faded out. Something *new* had faded in – much as a photograph develops in a chemical bath.

It was all hauntingly familiar, along with the *thump thump thump* of the music beat that vibrated through his chest.

As Guidry watched, distracted from Kate's delectable anus, another room – this one dark, dirty, and rank – had *superimposed* itself over the one in the house he'd known his entire life. The new room was smaller and, as its wall materialized, it trapped Kate/Andrew from their waist upward within its bricks. As the bricks grew more solid, they *replaced* Kate/Andrew and the poor Buds died a lingering, painful death, their screams silenced by the density of the wall. Finally, in a final insult, the remaining half of their conjoined body slid down the wall, and what was left of their viscera spread out across the bed.

Guidry considered himself most fortunate as he observed Budworld appearing around him. There had been an old, soiled bed in that alternate timeline – pretty much where the one in Mhari's old room had been – and he'd just so happened to have been kneeling down in the right place to avoid becoming part of the new building's structure.

He'd not been in that part of the sex club before – his activities had always been confined to the dance floor area – but the overbearing music and the stink of sex that permeated its back rooms were quite unmistakable.

Once the weird metamorphosis into a peculiar Real World/Budworld appeared to have settled down, and Guidry calculated that it was safe to do so, he ventured from the room, carefully stepping around the dead, bloodied half of Kate/Andrew. Although he'd gotten used to being publically naked, Guidry felt incredibly vulnerable as he made his way over the threshold and on to the dingy back rooms of the sex club.

As his eyes adjusted to the poor light, Guidry made out a long hallway that seemed to go on for miles before disappearing among its own darkness. The hallway was peppered here and there with randomly spaced doors, some of which were wide open. From the inky shadows within, Guidry heard quiet moans and the faint sound of pitiful sobs.

He walked on.

Behind one of the doors was a young woman chained to the bare brick wall. It was difficult to tell her exact age, as her swollen face was bloated and bloodied, its skin split in several places al the way down to the bone. Her entire naked body was adorned with bruises – some dark blue and fresh, others the nasty yellow-green of age. A Bud sat on the floor below her with three snake-like dicks inserted deep into her vagina. The creature comprised a single body with one spectacular breast in its center, plus three pelvises, six legs, and the aforementioned triumvirate of penises. As the Bud idly fucked the barely conscious woman, it chewed on the toes of her left foot.

The chained woman groaned as she saw Guidry pass by, her dulled eyes begging him for help. Guidry considered doing intervening to do so as he paused by the door, but his more rational mind countered with: *what could I possibly do here?* He'd figured out enough to understand things had changed: either his entire timeline had dropped back that final fraction of a second to Budworld – *how he* still *hated that name!* – or Budworld's had somehow caught up with his. Either way, Guidry figured, the rules were bound to be different now.

Ashamed at his cowardice, Guidry walked on. And, as he witnessed the horrors behind the other doors, he understood the Buds must have been taking people from his timeline to feast upon for a long, long time. His mind turned to his lost prototype device – *#1* – and grasped the fact all of this was his fault entirely: the transportation of citizens between the two timelines had obviously been a two-way street.

Just how many humans had the Buds brought back to feed on?

That thought made Guidry shudder.

Here was a mother and small child, surrounded by a group of Buds. Each one of the creatures comprised four offshoots, their limbs tangled together to form an inescapable barrier. One of the Buds had what looked to be the rear end of another sticking out from its back, as if someone had run headlong into it and got stuck, while another had a large fetus growing sideways on its thigh. The mother's shoulders spasmed with heart-rending sobs as the Buds pulled her child – a boy of eight or nine – apart before her eyes and devoured his flesh with wet, noisy slurps.

Guidry realized then he had never seen a Bud eat before. He'd always figured they preferred to do it in private, or they had something akin to photosynthesis going on, what with their mutual energy-sharing and all.

How very wrong he'd been.

Another room had an elderly man sitting astride a male/female Bud, which had a third head and an arm sprouting from its abdomen. The old man bobbed up and down in a half-hearted attempt at coitus, with the Bud having to hold him upright to save him from falling off of its grotesque body. Upon closer inspection, Guidry saw the man was not elderly at all: he was a young man once in his prime, his features sunken, dried out, *drained*.

Mercifully, many of the other doors along that hellish hallway were closed, and only the cries and moans escaped to tug at Guidry's conscience.

Eventually, Guidry found the exit at the end of the hallway. It was unmarked and adjacent to a room in which an obese Bud with a dozen shriveled arms and legs jutting from its torso was hunched over two naked women strapped tightly to a filthy, blood-stained mattress. One of the women was already dead; the entirety of her skin and muscle was stripped from her front – neck to pubic mound – and pink-white bone glistened through the clotting blood. The other was very much alive and screamed against the red ball gag secured in her mouth. The grotesque Bud was occupied with eating her breasts; in a sick twist of etiquette, it sliced away the soft, fatty meat with a silver knife and fork before popping each morsel in to its blubbery mouth with a long, satisfied *mmmmmmmm*.

Sick to his stomach, Guidry was relieved to be out of the hallway and the twisted terrors it harbored. Sadly, his relief was short-lived as, to his dismay, outside in the streets beyond the sex club, the horrors continued.

There were many more victims of the superimposition of Budworld's timeline onto Guidry's: people he recognized as clients and employees of the brothel were trapped in the brick walls, roads, sidewalks, lampposts, and trees of the new world. Some were still alive and trapped by legs, arms, and lower bodies, and all cried out for help as they struggled in vain against the things that held them. Others were beyond help, absorbed by their heads and upper bodies into the solidified substance of Budworld.

For those human individuals who had – by pure fluke – managed to avoid that particular fate, there was little redemption to be had. Everywhere Guidry looked, Buds were chasing down and consuming people. All pretense and subtlety had been abandoned as the Buds were no longer content – or required to pretend – to sap their prey's energy through fucking. They tore into flesh, snapped bones, and sucked on succulent entrails with loud, lip smacking sounds that brought the acid sting of bile to Guidry's throat.

Yet, still the Buds fucked the humans – alive and dead – their warty pricks eating out flesh from the inside of mouths, cunts, asses, while diseased vaginas chewed through tongues, fingers, and the tough gristle of human cocks.

And, as the Buds feasted and fornicated upon the ravaged bodies with all the finesse of wild, rutting animals, their own grotesque forms grew rapidly and erupted with hideous offshoots. All about Guidry, the air filled with terrible screams that echoed through the dark streets, and blood flowed thickly along the gutters as people died their horrible, agonizing deaths.

Anxious for his own safety, Guidry remained in the shadows, his heart – *thump thump thump* – in time to the music beats that wafted from the club. He contemplated turning back, but feared for his life in the death riddled back rooms. He figured he could take his chances outside, possibly make it over to Kate/Andrew's apartment; it wasn't as if they'd be needing it any time soon.

Occasionally, the gaudy buildings around Guidry would fade out slightly; in their place, Guidry caught glimpses of the ghosts of the trees he'd grown up with. They'd flicker into semi-existence, like the bones in one's hand when held close to a light bulb, and then out again. Even the sex club faded just enough for him to see the magnificent facade of his family home, as if it were fighting a losing battle against the Budworld overlay for the rights to its timeline.

The nebulous outline of the Guidry house flickered out, and was gone for Guidry understood was for the final time; one way or another, the world as he had known it was completely and irrevocably embedded within the Buds' world now.

A group of Buds ran by – seven, maybe eight, it was hard to tell in the gloom, and they had so many offshoots – each one clutched lumps of fresh, bloodied meat in their hands. Some ate as they ran, and Guidry saw some of the chunks of raw flesh had skinned arms, hands, toes.

One of the Buds slowed up by the shadows concealing Guidry. It was a two-man creature joined at the side of the head and hip, and whom sported a row of a dozen magnificently erect penises along its spine. It also had a third, lively head between its buttocks and a pair of twisted, crippled legs dangling from its neck. The Bud's eyes met with Guidry's, and a flicker of recognition flashed with malevolence.

Guidry froze.

"It's alright – they won't kill you," a soft voice whispered in his ear, so close, Guidry felt the warm breath that accompanied it. The two-man Bud cracked a crooked smile across its bloodied mouth and ran off to join its companions; they had had pinned down a middle-aged woman and were fucking and eviscerating her in the doorway to one of the sex stores; the unfortunate woman wailed blue murder and tried her damndest to fight them off.

Sickened, Guidry turned to face the voice; the acrid whiff of decay turned his stomach.

"Hello again, Wildus!" Mhari whispered.

Guidry's own voice abandoned him. The best he could do was to attempt a smile, even though Mhari's ghoulish appearance and vile stink made him want to run.

"They – *we* need you alive."

Guidry looked at her, dumbstruck. "You do?"

"You're the only one who can rebuild the time machine, dummy." She gave Guidry a playful tap on the chest with her middle arm.

"*And* the only one who can find us more timelines," Mhari's twin head added through torn, ragged lips.

"Since this was the last one *we* could find using your device," Mhari continued, "and we'll have consumed it very soon, as you can see."

So that was it, Guidry thought.

The Buds had been absorbing alternate timelines, feasting on their inhabitants, and moving on. It certainly explained his discovery of time travel extending only three one thousandths of a second – the Buds had eaten all the others!

Mhari wrapped a rough, damp hand around Guidry's dick. He felt it twitch at her touch; it was sore, overly sensitive, and the pressure of her hand squeezed out a dollop of stinking pus, but still it aroused him.

"Looks like someone has the STD." Mhari smiled down at Guidry's swelling prick, which resembled a grotesque Christmas log – stick a plastic robin on the thing, and the effect would be complete.

"*Yeah.*" Guidry let out a sigh as Mhari stroked the rough skin; the warts' tiny eyes winked up at him.

Mhari pulled Guidry toward her. Despite the smell wafting over her shoulder from the dead guy on her back, Guidry yielded and allowed Mhari to maneuver his oozing dick up into her pussy.

"We've all been looking forward to the Big Catch-Up." The twin head said as Mhari's hands gripped Guidry's buttocks and urged him to thrust; she pushed hard on him and snaked a forefinger into his asshole to coax him to come. "We've been *ever so* hungry."

At once, Guidry felt the energy drain from his body – one muscle at a time; his body was closing down.

The Buds had been feeding on him, 'Chelle, and their clients all along, sucking out their life force (*their souls?*) bit by bit as they'd so expertly played at being passive sex slaves. Obviously, they'd eschewed their natural instincts to rip their prey apart and guzzle down every morsel of flesh and drop of fluid – all in the cause of biding their time, adapting their behavior to feed like parasites designed to not eat the whole animal – just a little of it at a time.

But, Guidry's world was now the Buds' world, and all bets were off.

IF THERE'S A PROLOGUE, THERE HAS TO BE AN EPILOGUE

Wildus Guidry had been right all along.

The device he'd built had indeed been indicating a countdown of sorts, and with each leap back in time, he'd inadvertently accelerated the shortening of the gap between the Buds' timeline and his own.

The Buds (*and he'd hate that word 'till his dying day*) fed from each other and, as such, dwelled in an energy closed circuit. So, taking into account the Law of Diminishing Returns, the only way they could possibly survive was by absorbing alternate timelines, enslaving the populace they found there, and taking what sustenance they needed in spite of the dire consequences for the indigenous species.

The Buds would keep Guidry alive long enough for him to create a new device to open up fresh, new timelines in which they could sate their perverse appetites for both sex and flesh.

And, as it turned out, that was going to be a long, long time...

END

ABOUT THE AUTHOR

James H. longmore hails originally from Doncaster, a mining town in the south of Yorkshire, Northern England; he relocated with his family to Houston, Texas in 2010. James boasts an honors degree in Zoology and a former career background in sales, marketing, and business.

He is an accomplished, published author (and publisher), and ghostwriter of popular fiction - he writes across a wide range of genres and subjects: novels, shorts, and screenplays. He has written and directed award-winning short movies, is an affiliate member of the Horror Writer's Association, and has run/hosted the popular podcast/radio show *The New Panic Room* since early 2016,

In addition, James is the founder and owner of the indie publisher, *HellBound Books Publishing LLC* (est. 2016), which publishes horror, bizarro, and a whole manner of dark fiction.

http://www.panicroomradio.com

http://www.hellboundbookspublishing.com

James H Longmore

ALSO BY JAMES H LONGMORE

TENEBRION

"The Devil's in the detail."

Amateur filmmakers inadvertently invoke a demon when they break into an abandoned school to perform and film an authentic Black Mass for their entry into a short movie competition.

Dave Priestley and his crew film in Watsonville elementary school – the site of a horrific tragedy nine years before.

Tenebrion – the malevolent demon of darkness – makes preparations of its own within the dark recesses of Hell. The demon requires a specific set of circumstances and sacrifices to rend a fissure between the worlds and set free its brethren; it has manipulated humans for centuries to put things into place, and the moviemakers are the unfortunate, final pieces of its nefarious puzzle.

Priestley, ever the stickler for authenticity and detail, accidentally sets free the denizen of Hell. And while Priestley and his skeptical friends attempt to return Tenebrion to the pit of Hades, it hunts them all down – one by one – for inclusion in its hellish gateway.

AND THEN YOU DIE:

Following a drunken, hedonistic night out in New Orleans, highly successful businesswoman and sexual deviant, Claire Jepson, accidentally soils herself in her car. The resulting excrement comes to life as a sardonic fecal spirit, and not only dishes out a gruesome death to Claire's unfaithful, gold-digging fiancé, but also thwarts a kidnap/murder plot by her employees. It then introduces Claire to a world of depraved pleasures beyond her imagination.

A year later, the errant spirit has spiraled wildly out of control - its insatiable appetite for perverted sex and human flesh and has destroyed Claire's life. Then, to her horror, Claire discovers the fecal spirit must consume her unborn child to attain immortality; she must return to the seedy underbelly of the Big Easy in a heart-pounding race against time to confront the spirit's creator - a high priest of an ancient, deadly order, who is the only one who can put a stop to the spirit's murderous intentions. A wicked, fast-paced story laced with tongue-in-cheek, dark humor, which is at the same time incredibly erotic and stomach churning. Most definitely not one to be read whilst eating!

PEDE:

An affectionate homage to the creature feature! The once luxurious Mountainview Spa Hotel in the heart of California's Coachella valley lies decaying, abandoned and heavily boarded up - the site of a radioactive, "dirty" bomb explosion five years' previously. Zoology Professor, Jane Lucas, harbors a lifelong phobia of *Scolopendra gigantea,* the Giant Centipede, despite being the world's leading authority on the creature. Following the savage deaths of two teenagers who broke into the hotel to cavort in the natural underground spa and the discovery of centipede remains almost three times natural size, the professor teams up with four of her students to investigate.

Their expedition soon becomes a fight for survival when they're trapped inside the hotel with a gang of violent thugs and a voracious swarm of oversized centipedes that infest the place - and then discover another creature even more terrifying is hunting in the Mountainview's deserted hallways: a centipede of impossibly monstrous proportions… ravenous and desperate to feed.

FLANAGAN

"The Devil's Rejects meets Fifty Shades – heart-pounding, gut-wrenching, sexy as all hell, and with a twist you'll never see coming!"

Meet the Sewells, an all-American couple; happily married for ten years, respected high school teachers, still crazy about one another, and with a mutually-shared dark side.

During their annual Spring Break vacation to recharge batteries and reconnect, the Sewells are waylaid by a perverse gang of misfits in the one-horse, North Texas town of Flanagan.

Taken hostage to be the focus of the gang's twisted games, the Sewells are brutalized into performing vicious physical, sexual, and emotional acts upon one another, until events take an unexpected turn, triggered by an unintentional death. As their circumstances descend into the worse nightmare imaginable, the Sewells find themselves involved in an altogether different situation...

THE EROTIC ODYSSEY OF COLTON FORSHAY

Colton Forshay dreams himself into a bizarre sexual dystopia - a world in which nothing is as it should be, it alternately rains semen and menstrual blood, sickening sex acts and sexual violence are the norm, and the currency is deviant sexual acts.

In this dream world, Colton inexplicably finds he has gotten his dog pregnant and his wife is brutally murdered as a contestant on a popular TV show.

At first disturbed, then intrigued - and shamefully aroused - by his dreams of the other world, Colton is drawn in deeper and begins to spend more time there with the help of sleeping pills. His real-world wife forces Colton to see a psychiatrist, who encourages him to explore the dream world. And thus, our hero embarks on an odyssey with his dog/son, Eric, to discover the disturbing truth behind his dream world.

There, Colton gets caught up with the resistance, who believe the government - lead by a mysterious, telepathic ocelot - controls the people by means of dreams of another realm, which sounds uncannily like his actual world.

The storyline alternates between Colton's real and fantasy dream worlds, and the two become inexorably blurred until Colton unearths a disturbing truth not entirely against the perverse tastes he's developed.

This is fantastical tale populated by a whole host of bizarre characters, set in an incredibly peculiar world. Chock-full of startling, sexy imagery and told with incredibly dark humor, Colton Forshay is a bizarro tale both engaging and disturbing.

<u>BLOOD AND KISSES</u>

"Think of what late greats James Herbert and Richard Laymon may have given birth to had they ever collaborated" - Richard Chizmar
The definitive short story collection from James H Longmore - an eclectic mix of dark horror, bizarro and *Twilight Zone* style tales of the downright disturbing. Welcome to the long-awaited collection from the writer of horror novels *'Pede* and *Tenebrion*; a foreword by Richard Chizmar (co-author of *Gwendy's Button Box* with Stephen King), 18 short stories, 5 flash fiction, and a poem - all skin-crawling, soul-shredding tales of the darkest things that skulk among the night's inky shadows and of the everyday gone horribly awry.
Discover the implication of technology becoming self-aware, enjoy the acquaintance of a charismatic new pastor promising his flock a brand new place to worship his God, spend a little time in the company of a nice young man who is inexorably caught up in his home town's terrible secret. Then, there's Cupid's revelation he's never experienced love, we discover that very emotion alive and not so well among the ruins of a post-zombie apocalyptic world, and bear witness to childhood innocence forever destroyed in a distant, war-torn city.
Observe, too any unsavory individual's obsession with the ever-elusive snuff movie, and join an elderly bunch of forgetful sleuths out to solve the mystery of brutal deaths that occur with alarming regularity at their memory care facility.
Now, have you ever considered what may happen should you have the misfortune to bump into your family's doppelgangers on a long, tedious road trip? And, can you even begin to imagine being the doting father who finally realizes the apple of his eye's true identity, or the parents

who spend what is left of their crumbling lives waiting by a silent telephone for news of their addict son?

There is more, Dear Reader, much, much more; for within the pages we have devils, demons and ghosts, lycanthropes, and demi-gods, all rubbing nefarious shoulders with the most vile of Hell's offspring, who have slithered up from the netherworld to doff their caps and wish us all the sweetest of dreams…

FEEDER

A deliciously bizarro, darkly disturbing peek into the world of gainers and feeders: grotesquely obese individuals and those people who facilitate their growth for the lascivious pleasure of both parties. The heroine of the piece, Novella, Embarks upon a journey into the dreadful netherworld that dwells within the obese, fleshy folds of a woman especially engorged for the perverted delights of her Internet audience. Aided and abetted by a former feeder, she fights to escape before the grim portal closes and she's trapped forever in the ghastly realm of fat, flesh, and death most gruesome.

I AM JOE'S UNWANTED PENIS

A darkly comedic tribute to the much-loved Reader's Digest series *'I am Joe's…(insert body part here)'* and a bizarre parody of the Bruce Jenner story, *I Am Joe's Unwanted Penis* is told from the point of view of a penis discarded as a man is surgically transformed into a woman.

Upon learning if his high-profile previous owner's regret at having made the transformation, the penis embarks upon a perilous journey for them to be reunited - aided and abetted by a motley, wonderfully personable and, engaging selection of other discarded body parts.

In parts grotesque, laugh-out-loud funny, and undeniably poignant, in others, *I Am Joe's Unwanted Penis* is a buddy-story absolutely like no other!

James H Longmore

**A HellBound Books LLC
Publication 2021**

www.hellboundbookspublishing.com

Printed in the United States of America